Modern Fairies, Dwarves, Goblins & Other Nasties

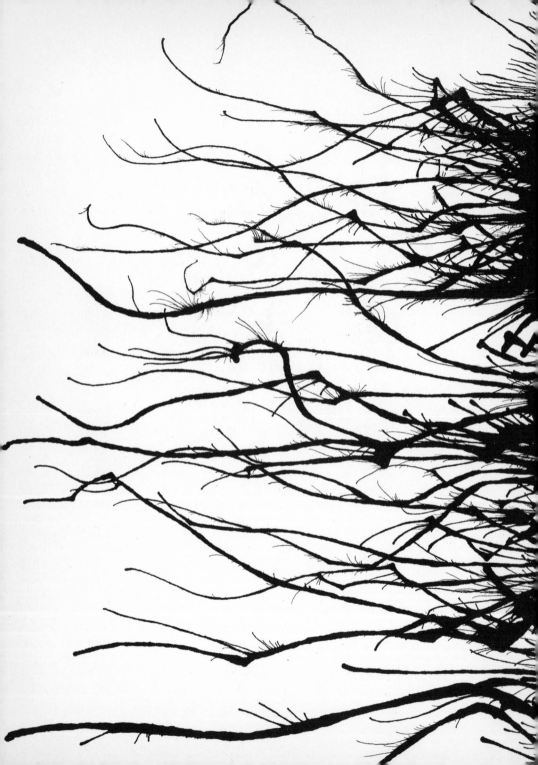

Modern Fairies, Dwarves, Goblins & Other Nasties

A Practical Guide by
Miss Edythe McFate

As told to **Lesley M. M. Blume**
Illustrated by **David Foote**

Alfred A. Knopf   New York

For Greta, the sweetest little hobgoblin in New York City
—L.M.M.B.

For my lovely Lauren
—D.F.

THIS IS A BORZOI BOOK PUBLISHED BY ALFRED A. KNOPF

Text copyright © 2010 by Lesley M. M. Blume
Illustrations copyright © 2010 by David Foote
All rights reserved. Published in the United States by Alfred A. Knopf,
an imprint of Random House Children's Books, a division of Random House, Inc., New York.
Knopf, Borzoi Books, and the colophon are registered trademarks of Random House, Inc.
Visit us on the Web! www.randomhouse.com/kids
Educators and librarians, for a variety of teaching tools,
visit us at www.randomhouse.com/teachers
Library of Congress Cataloging-in-Publication Data
Blume, Lesley M. M.
Modern fairies, dwarves, goblins, and other nasties : a practical guide / by Miss Edythe McFate ;
as told to Lesley M. M. Blume ; illustrated by David Foote. — 1st ed.
    p.   cm.
Summary: A compendium of practical information and cautionary tales about fairies and other similar magical creatures that might be encountered in modern cities like New York, intended to help the child who may come into contact with them.
ISBN 978-0-375-86203-8 (trade) — ISBN 978-0-375-96203-5 (lib. bdg.) —
ISBN 978-0-375-85493-4 (pbk.) — ISBN 978-0-375-89702-3 (e-book)
[1. Fairies—Fiction. 2. New York (N.Y.)—Fiction.] I. Foote, David, ill. II. Title.
PZ7.B62567Mo 2010
[Fic]—dc22
2010004961
The text of this book is set in 14-point Seria.
The illustrations in this book were created using a Victorian dip pen and black ink on paper.
Printed in the United States of America
September 2010
10 9 8 7 6 5 4 3 2 1
First Edition

Contents

Introduction

My name is Miss Edythe McFate, and once you've read my practical guide to modern fairies, you will never see the world around you in the same way again.

You may think that fairies are make-believe or extinct like dinosaurs. You also probably think of all fairies as lovely winged creatures, frolicking around in bluebell fields, singing and dancing and granting wishes.

If so, you're wrong on all counts.

Firstly, fairies are very much alive today, and they are everywhere—in your city, in your backyard, even in your kitchen cupboards. In the old days, most fairies did live in the countryside, and some of them still do, of course. But many fairies also dwell in cities and towns and live startlingly modern lives.

Secondly, fairies come in many different forms. The majority of fairies indeed resemble tiny winged humans, but the fairy family includes goblins, trolls, dwarves, brownies, and countless other creatures. Each breed can have hundreds of sub-breeds: in fact, the family tree for the winged fairy species alone would have over ten thousand branches.

Finally—and most importantly: while some fairies are indeed pretty and sweet-tempered, others can be quite nasty or even dangerous.

What all fairy breeds have in common: magical powers that can be used to do something nice for you—or ruin your life forever. Some fairies are shape-shifters or curse-wielders; others are hypnotists and kidnappers. Sometimes you can outsmart them, but nine times out of ten, they'll get the better of you.

In this guidebook, you will find heaps of practical advice on how to tell a good fairy from a bad one and how to spot a "fairy ring"; you will learn the difference between dwarves and trolls (one species is far deadlier than the other) and how to defend yourself against fairies who would do you harm. I've also included eight cautionary stories about children your age who've had some astonishing encounters with fairies. Each of these tales deals with a different type of fairy, and I'm warning you: some of the stories aren't pretty. In fact, several are quite terrifying. But every single one of these stories is true, so I'd advise you to read them all and pay close attention in case you find yourself in similar situations.

Forewarned is forearmed, I always say.

And to prove that fairies really have adapted to the most modern environments, the stories that I'm retelling happened right smack in the middle of bustling, ultra-modern, taxi-and-people-filled New York City, where I have lived since I was born.

Like most Americans, many fairy species came from someplace else in the world, and they often arrived on the same ships that landed at New York's famous Ellis Island. It might be hard to imagine now, but years ago, New York City was filled with woods and streams and fields—just the sort of place that all kinds of fairies would like to call home.

So, like the human immigrants, hundreds of fairies settled right in, and as the decades and centuries passed, what
would become the City of Steel slowly swallowed up the fields
and dammed up the streams and devoured the woods where
the original immigrant fairies had made their new homes.
Did they leave? Some of them did. But others stayed on, and
unlike their distant cousins in the countryside, today's urban
fairies are in daily contact with their human neighbors. After
all, New Yorkers live practically on top of each other, and the
city's fairies are no exception.

You might think that all of this contact would make the
fairies tame and friendly, but actually the opposite is true. Fairies
are extremely private creatures, and they often become very
resentful when spied on or interfered with or rankled in any
way. Living in such close proximity to so many species means
that you will have a hundred times as many opportunities to
offend nearby fairies—however unknowingly. Plus, the more
sinister types of fairies have historically found many uses for
innocent children, and city living affords them the pick of the
litter.

My guide and stories will help to protect you. The more
you know about fairies, the more likely you are to attract and
befriend the lovely ones—and the better you'll be able to
protect yourself against those who wish you ill.

You might ask: Why should I listen to you?

Allow me to share my credentials. I have spent almost

my entire life—seven decades—studying the ways of every known species of fairy. I've read nearly everything ever written on the subject, from crumbling ancient manuscripts in Scottish castles to pencil-scribbled descriptions of fairy sightings by Kansas farmwives. I've had countless first-hand encounters with fairies, from goblins to mermaids to winged sprites. Like the children in the following stories, I have what's called fairy sight, which means that I can see fairies everywhere I go, whether they want me to spot them or not.

You might envy me, but let me assure you: fairy sight is a mixed blessing. I can see a fantastical fairy wedding taking place in an ivy patch while you would unwittingly stump right past it. I would also notice, for example, that the fat fireflies hovering about in your backyard are not flies at all: they are disguised Helio fairies, who wake up and glow every evening at dusk. But I also see hideous goblins hunkered down in city alleys, eating neighborhood cats, and am often treated to the view of the fanged Noctis fairies, swirling about in the nighttime air on the backs of bats, scavenging for dead squirrels and mice.

But you will learn about me and my own fairy encounters later.

The bottom line: no one knows more about the wayward natures, properties, and habits of fairies than me, and I've chosen to share this information with you.

5

Read this book all at once or a few chapters and entries at a time; carry it with you to reference it on the run.

By the book's end, you too will be an expert on the modern fairy world.

Miss Edythe McFate
New York City, 2010

How to Tell a Good Fairy
from a Bad One

This is an extremely important entry and so is the next one; read them carefully, because this information could save your life someday.

Over the centuries, people have come up with countless spells, chants, potions, and strategies to help you recognize a bad fairy and protect yourself from it. Most of them are pretty far-fetched. One potion recipe even calls for hair from the hind leg of a satyr (a creature that is half man, half horse), which you're supposed to wear in a brass locket around your neck.

Forget about such nonsense.

Here is the easiest and most reliable trick in the world: if you encounter a fairy, place a penny on the floor right away.

If the penny glows blue, you're probably safe.

If the penny glows green—or worse, black—run away immediately, and don't look back for a second.

If only the children in some of the tales ahead had known about this trick.

How to Protect Yourself
from a Dangerous Fairy

In the past, people used some very odd things as charms to ward off pesky or dangerous fairies. Ancient books call for the use of churchyard mold or a pig's head. One strange recipe calls for a mixture of "myrrh, wine, white incense, and shavings from an agate stone."

None of these things are exactly easy to locate in a supermarket today.

Luckily, some old-fashioned fairy charms are still easy to find, such as daisies. Tied into a chain, they become especially powerful. To protect you while you're asleep, roll up a sock and put it under your bed. No one knows why this keeps fairies away, but it does; maybe it has something to do with the stink of a dirty sock. Fairies are usually quite fastidious, and most of them cannot abide human stinks. Wearing your socks inside out will protect you on the go.

If a bad fairy catches you by surprise and you aren't wearing any socks and no daisies are available, do not panic. Just immediately say the following:

North,
South,

East,
West.
Sun rise,
Sun set.

Repeat this easy-to-remember chant over and over, louder each time. It sounds silly, I agree, but it casts a spell on most breeds of fairies: when they hear it, they're forced to take backward steps. It's actually quite fascinating to watch this happen, but don't stick around too long to gape. Once they've backed up far enough, get away from there as quickly as your legs can carry you.

Gifts to Give Today's Fairies

Fairies love getting presents.

It is a good idea to leave fairy presents out even if you're not sure that one lives near you. A gift may prevent a mischievous fairy from interfering in your affairs; better yet, it may turn an appreciative fairy into your protector.

And if you're very lucky, a fairy may repay your kindness by letting you have a glimpse of him or her, even if you don't have fairy sight.

Old books and manuscripts instruct you to offer things like gold pieces, silver-winged dragonflies, and brass keys—expensive items that are not easy to come by today.

But there are many things in your own closets, drawers, and kitchen cupboards that make perfect gifts for fairies.

For example, they like anything shaped like little animals, such as goldfish crackers, animal crackers, gummi bears, and even gummi worms. They're also partial to those charm bracelets and necklaces, and they are cuckoo about lockets; anything that has a secret or private compartment intrigues them.

Next time your family eats corn on the cob for dinner, save some of the silk when you husk the corn beforehand. Leave it out for the fairies; they weave dresses and rugs and hammocks out of it.

In the old days, people left little bowls of water on their hearths for fairy mothers to come and bathe their babies. This is still a nice thing to do for them. If you don't have a hearth (meaning a fireplace), you can leave the bowl on a windowsill—preferably one bathed in moonlight. Make sure that it's the nicest bowl you can find, and the water should be warm, but not too hot.

An extra treat for fairy mothers: place a flower next to the bowl (preferably a rose, carnation, or chrysanthemum). Fairy mothers will place their babies on the flower petals to dry.

Sometimes fairies will reward such gestures by giving you nice presents in return, as you will see in the next story.

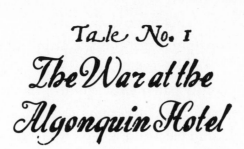

Tale No. 1
The War at the Algonquin Hotel

You've likely heard of the famous Algonquin Hotel on Manhattan's West 44th Street, which sits like a tired, dignified old man with his back turned to the nearby carnival of Times Square.

There was always something shady and calm about the Algonquin, which makes sense when you think about it. After all, hundreds of years ago, a magnificent oak tree lived where the hotel now stands.

But then along came settlers, who eventually decided that they needed hotels with things like claw-footed bathtubs and room service. And so they raised their axes, and many thousands of *chops* and *hacks* later, the magnificent oak tree was gone and its wood was made into the frame of the Algonquin Hotel.

It used to be quite a peculiar place. When you pushed through the heavy glass-and-oak doors into the lobby, the air grew heavier and wreathed around your shoulders like a fur shawl. This was all very strange until you realized that this is what it feels like when time is slowing down.

If you needed proof that this was happening, you could have watched the old grandfather clock facing the concierge desk, which sighed rather than chimed; its spindly hands circled the yellowing clock face more slowly than the hands of every other clock in the world, and yet somehow the time was always right. A teacup that fell in the Algonquin took longer to hit the floor than anyplace else in the world.

The Algonquin still managed to run like a normal hotel, despite the honey-in-winter pace of life there. Somehow towels got washed and pressed and arrived with lavender sweetness in all of the bathrooms; crisp newspapers appeared outside the door of each room at dawn; hot meals were turned out of the kitchen in a timely manner, although usually in need of a little salt.

But no one at the Algonquin could figure out exactly how things ran so smoothly. Not the ancient, white-gloved waiters, most of whom were as old as the grandfather clock; nor the kitchen staff; nor the chambermaids; and certainly not the sleepy, disheveled manager of the hotel, Mr. Harold Kneebone. When pressed on the subject, Mr. Kneebone would always say:

"Who can say for sure what makes the clock tick, or the sun rise and set, or the wheat grow? These things just happen, that's all."

And then, more often than not, he would nestle his face into his forearms and sail off into a soulful, sweet little nap.

However, two Algonquin residents understood *exactly* why the establishment ran like clockwork.

The first was a big, fat orange cat with yellow eyes named Mathilde, who lived in a little diorama of a room carved into one of the lobby walls. A golden-lettered wooden sign dangled above the cubby and proclaimed:

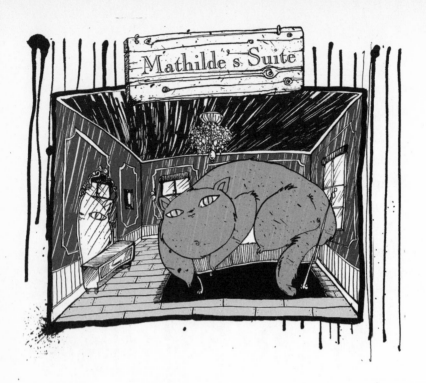

And the second resident in the know was Olive, the eight-year-old daughter of the hotel chef.

Olive was especially good at two things: making fruit salads and keeping secrets. Mathilde was her best friend, and when fruit-salad duty didn't keep Olive in the kitchen, the girl and the cat sat in their favorite corner of the lobby behind a potted palm.

One evening, the old headwaiter peeked around the palm to see what they were up to. Their heads were turning from side to side in unison.

"What are you looking at, an invisible tennis match?" asked the headwaiter warily.

"Nope," said Olive.

"Well, what, then?" pressed the headwaiter.

Mathilde settled her chin onto her paws, her yellow eyes tracing invisible mice darting across the floor.

"Just looking around," Olive responded mysteriously.

Not that the headwaiter would have believed Olive if she'd told him the truth: that she and Mathilde were watching brownies.

BROWNIE

Not many people today are familiar with brownies, indisputedly the friendliest species of fairy. Tiny, wingless creatures, brownies wear hats made from nutshells and dapper little three-piece suits and have a gentle sort of magic mostly used for practical jokes.

Usually found in places where large operations are going on, like factories and, of course, hotels, brownies always like to run things—whether they've been invited to help or not. They adhere to strict routines, which makes them excellent workers. But be warned: *nothing* makes a brownie behave more badly than a disrupted routine.

In the old days, brownies lived in trees and when they died, their spirits became one with those trees. Generations of brownies had lived in the Algonquin oak tree before it got chopped up and made into the hotel itself. Since then, the descendants of the original Algonquin brownies had adopted the hotel as their home, and as you probably guessed, those brownies—not the old waiters or Mr. Kneebone—were the ones running the establishment so well.

In fact, the brownies took great pride in their hoteling skills.

They preferred to remain invisible and anonymous to avoid interference, but Olive had been born with fairy sight. But even though she could see them, she couldn't understand their language, which sounded like the peeps of newborn chicks. Maybe Mathilde could understand them. We'll never know for sure. Yet over the years, Olive had become the brownies' friend, and she worked hard to keep them happy.

Because when the Algonquin brownies weren't happy, things went quite wrong around the hotel.

Take, for example, that time the florist brought tiger lilies to decorate the lobby instead of the usual forget-me-nots.

Brownies love forget-me-nots.

They hate tiger lilies.

Later that morning, fat Mr. Arbuckle, permanent tenant of room 42, came downstairs for his breakfast.

"Six eggs over easy, four pieces of white toast with butter and marmalade, ten pieces of well-done bacon, and coffee  with cream and sugar," he called as he lumbered across the dining room and lowered himself into his usual chair at his usual table.

Bang!

Splat!

Mr. Arbuckle's chair buckled beneath him and he crashed to the floor.

The waiters discovered shortly thereafter that the fourth leg of every chair in the room had been sawed in half.

Suddenly every tiger-lily-filled vase in the lobby crashed to the floor, sending shards and petals and water flying across the marble. When Olive saw a troop of brownies heading for the china cabinet, she ran up 44th Street to the flower shop.

"Come right away," she shouted at the florist. "Everyone at the Algonquin is horribly allergic to the tiger lilies. Bring forget-me-nots as fast as you can."

The tiger lilies were snatched off the floor and thrown out into the street; the forget-me-nots were stuffed into mop buckets and empty soup cans until new vases could be bought. The waiters took a badly needed tea break in the Rose Bar.

When the waiters came back out, each of the sawed-up dining room chairs somehow had four perfectly fit legs again.

Everyone but Mr. Arbuckle marveled at the miracle.

"Madness!" he shouted, rubbing an ice pack on his rather bruised bottom. "I demand that you find the culprit! Who is responsible?"

Mr. Kneebone resumed his post behind the concierge desk.

"Who can say for sure," he yawned, exhausted from the day's ordeal. "These things just happen, that's all."

And he sank into a grateful late-morning slumber.

Please don't get the wrong idea about the Algonquin brownies.

For the most part, they really are very sweet creatures. They just happen to be particular.

You might think that Olive had a very hard job to do, keeping the brownies happy. But understand this: the brownies looked after Olive as well.

They chanted sweet little spells while she slept to make her grow up pretty; they mixed special chestnut honey into her morning tea that made her hair thick as rope.

Each year on her birthday, they turned a fruit crate into a puppy for an hour or so, until the barking started to draw

23

attention. When Olive cried, the brownies turned her tears into rosewater drops and bottled them in pretty perfume jars and hid the jars away for later, because everyone knows that rosewater tears dabbed on the face of an old woman will make her young again.

The brownies loved Olive as much as they loved orderliness and industry, and she loved them too.

So, now that we've cleared that up, let's return to our story, which is about to take an interesting turn.

Progress is a hungry thing, and eventually it hunts down even the most resistant holdouts.

In this case, it arrived at the Algonquin in the form of Mr. Rex Runcible.

This Mr. Runcible stomped in through the glass-and-oak front doors and planted himself in the middle of the lobby, hands on his hips, mustache twitching, nose crinkled as though he smelled stinky cheese. He glared down at Mr. Kneebone, who slept in a happy little puddle of drool on the front desk.

"Wake up, you old billy goat," ordered Mr. Runcible, swatting Mr. Kneebone with his hat.

Mr. Kneebone snorted and woke up with a start. "Can I help you, sir?" he asked drowsily.

"Who's the manager here?" demanded Mr. Runcible.

"I am," replied Mr. Kneebone.

"You mean, you *were*," snapped Mr. Runcible. "You're fired. Good night and good luck to you."

A staff meeting was called. All of the hotel workers crammed into the lobby. All two hundred brownies were in attendance as well, standing on the moldings near the ceiling. Olive sat behind the potted palm next to Mathilde's suite and patted the orange cat nervously.

Mr. Runcible stood on a chair.

"I just bought the Algonquin from the old owner," he shouted. "And I intend to drag this dump out of the dark ages and into the modern world—starting now. All of you had better shape up or ship out. Big changes are coming."

The second his little speech was over, the glass-and-oak front doors swung open and in marched a small army of construction workers. They tore the front doors off the hinges and stuck power drills into the floor, sending chunks of marble flying everywhere. Then they piled up the lobby's furniture and hacked it up with axes.

And in the meantime, something else began to happen, something quiet and strange, something that no one noticed amidst the noise and chaos.

The hands of the old grandfather clock started to move faster.

As the workers tore the paintings from the walls and threw them on the floor, the clock's hands moved faster still. And when the workers pried up the oak wall panels with crowbars, the clock hands had almost caught up with the hands of the clocks in the world outside.

Olive looked up. All two hundred brownies stood like statues on the ceiling molding, paralyzed by the sight of the horrific destruction below. Several workers below hauled a vat of cement into the lobby and set it down in front of Mathilde's suite. Those workers laughed at the golden-lettered sign and pulled out Mathilde's precious little bed; one of them stepped on it, splintering it to pieces. Cement was mixed; Spackle knives were poised.

I'm sure you can guess what happened next.

Within minutes, Mathilde's suite was gone.

You would think that it would be hard to hear anything in that room over the drills and the ripping sounds and noise coming in from the street. But as the workers cemented up the cat's cubby, a shrill chant rose above the din.

And for the first time in her life, Olive understood the brownies' language. They said one word, over and over again:

"It will be business as usual around here," Mr. Runcible told the startled hotel customers, his face stretched into an unnatural-looking rubbery grin.

But no one believed him, and they were right not to.

When the workers left at sunset, a tense quiet settled over the shredded lobby. Olive sat in the corner, trying to glue Mathilde's bed back together while the cat watched with great concern.

By this time, the grandfather clock was ticking away so rapidly that it swayed, and it shook with noisy chimes as each hour passed.

And then, at midnight, on the twelfth stroke, the clock made a terrible noise, as though choking on nuts and bolts.

The face of the clock flew open and tiny springs shot out everywhere.

Rat-tat-tat-tat! Ping-ping-ping! Zzzzzing!

Olive heard gleeful cheers and shrieks: a team of brownies was climbing triumphantly down the side of the clock.

The war for the Algonquin had begun.

House phones began to ring in the lobby. Mr. Runcible answered them, juggling three or four receivers at a time.

"Yes? There's a *what* in room 33? A hog? That's impossible. All right, I'll send someone up right away."

And then:

"Hello? What? It's snowing in your room? You must be crazy." He shouted to no one in particular: "Turn up the thermostat in room 15!"

Just then, the elevator doors opened and out ran the hog from room 33. It tore about the lobby in crazy circles, stopping only to make a fine smelly barnyard mess in the corner. Mr. Runcible let out a squeal himself and leaped up onto the concierge counter. Olive and Mathilde chased the hog into the Rose Bar, just in time to see a brownie deftly turn it back into a barstool with a pig-leather seat.

At dawn, when the local paperboy wheeled his newspaper cart through the front entrance, he stumbled upon a peculiar scene, even by the standards of New York City.

"Thank heavens you're here," hollered Mr. Runcible, still

huddled on top of the concierge counter. All
of the waiters stood about the lobby as though
rooted to the floor.

"What's going
on?" asked the paperboy,
backing toward the entrance.

"We're all glued to the floor," yelled the
headwaiter. "Give us a hand, won't you, young man?"

But the paperboy fled—although his cart remained
steadfast in the lobby floor, which was indeed covered in
invisible glue. No one could budge an inch until noon, when
the glue suddenly dried and cracked around their feet and
Mr. Runcible's construction workers could come in and chip
everyone free.

⟨⟨⟨⟩⟩⟩ ⟨⟨⟨⟩⟩⟩ ⟨⟨⟨⟩⟩⟩

The war raged for days.

Strange molds and vines grew from the carpets; a waterfall of honey cascaded down the mail chute; a gang of yowling one-eyed alley cats appeared and tore up all of the feather pillows in the fourth-floor rooms. The hot taps ran orange juice and cold taps ran turpentine.

Then the brownies directed their attention to the construction equipment, turning the drills to quivering Jell-O molds and the crowbars into greasy strips of bacon. They unscrewed the heads of hammers and made sure that there were plenty of fleas in the workers' caps.

But each morning new equipment replaced the old, and more workers piled in through the front doors; Mr. Runcible directed his grunting, sweating army like a steel-fisted general. Gradually the oak disappeared entirely from the lobby walls (which received a bland coat of tapioca-colored paint), new pink-and-green carpets were stapled to the floors, the lobby took on an antiseptic-new smell, like plastic, and dull elevator music droned from newly installed stereo speakers near the ceiling.

Anything that looked old-fashioned or historic was chopped to pieces and tossed into a Dumpster outside.

The brownies were losing the war and they knew it.

Mr. Runcible was simply too determined to claim the soul of the hotel and would resort to anything. And when a man wants the soul of something but has no soul or conscience himself, he's almost always impossible to stop. You have to sacrifice some of your own soul to beat him, which means that he wins by that much more.

The last straw, which brought out the maximum cruelty in Mr. Rex Runcible: the brownies infested the man's mustache with worms. He shaved it off and retaliated by throwing nearly the entire hotel staff out into the street—most of whom hadn't even been outside in years.

"You can't stop progress," he shouted at their backs as they stood blinking and bewildered on the front sidewalk, suitcases in hand.

The last thing to go was the grandfather clock.

It chimed sadly to itself as it lay in the Dumpster on the curb, but no one could hear it over the angry honking horns and screaming sirens.

And soon the clock went silent.

Of course Mr. Runcible hired a new chef too: a jittery, bony young man whose specialty was weird modern dishes like short ribs with chocolate-and-nettle sauce. But before the new chef toured the kitchen, the brownies coated the floor in Crisco; the chef dutifully broke his nose and several other bones. So Olive and her dad were instructed to stay until the new chef could leave the hospital.

Olive's room was next to the kitchen. Actually, it was a big broom closet, with a makeshift bed and tiny window up near the ceiling, but it was cozy and warm and always smelled like croissants in the morning and steak béarnaise at night.

On her last night in the hotel, Olive packed quietly. She didn't have a suitcase because she had never been anywhere outside New York City. So she stuffed her clothes and possessions into a pillowcase instead.

One by one, the brownies came into her room: some under the crack beneath the door, others through the air vent. Soon all two hundred of them stood at her feet, staring up at her sadly, wringing their nutshell hats in their hands. Mathilde squeezed fatly through the slightly open door.

Olive sat on the floor, and several of the brownies climbed up onto her crossed legs. She worried for them. She knew that

her father would get a job in another hotel. These brownies, on the other hand, had been attached to the Algonquin oak for hundreds of years.

But there was no place for whimsical brownies in a hotel that stunk like plastic and was having its history and soul drained away in great gulps and gushes.

The brownies appeared to be reading her thoughts, and their little heads hung in grief and helplessness.

Then Olive had an idea. If there was no place for brownies in a modern Algonquin, maybe they could be moved someplace where *modernity hadn't happened yet.*

Someplace that looked like old New York, before the settlers came and wanted bathtubs and room service.

Olive could think of only one such place in Manhattan.

"I want you to be brave and follow me," she told the brownies. "I think I know a place where you can be happy again."

The brownies looked at each other apprehensively.

"You can't stay here," Olive said. "You know that I'm not like other humans. You can trust me. Now, are you coming?"

And then, all at once, the brownies stood up straight like cadets. One of them even saluted her.

Olive picked up Mathilde and nodded at the fairies gravely. Soon hundreds of years of history were behind them and they stood on the front sidewalk. Flashing neon lights burned through the midnight air and traffic still clogged the streets.

The brownies huddled in the hotel doorway.

"Looking back will only make you sad," Olive told them firmly.

And because Olive was indeed not like other humans and the brownies loved and trusted her, they swallowed their fear and followed her into Times Square.

Then the most extraordinary thing happened.

As Olive walked by the Dumpster on the curb, the Algonquin's discarded grandfather clock came back to life.

Its old face glowed blue and its gears creaked and groaned, and soon they turned with ease. Then they were whirring— and one by one the lights of Times Square flickered out. A hundred thousand bulbs popped and fizzled and turned to black; darkness seeped up the sides of the buildings. Cars ground to a halt. A man lighting a cigarette froze; even the flame from his match ceased to flicker and became an orange-yellow ribbon suspended in the air.

Time and progress stopped and respectfully bowed for the last march of the brownies.

The tiny parade wound up Seventh Avenue, two hundred creatures led by a small girl and a fat orange cat. They weaved around frozen pedestrians gleaming dully in the pale moonlight and around heaping trash bins and under blowing newspapers halted in mid-air.

Fifteen silent, still, dark city blocks later, Olive and Mathilde and the Algonquin brownies reached the entrance of tree-filled Central Park.

The brownies began to weep. Many of them had never even *seen* a tree, but all brownies belong to trees and most trees belong to brownies, and so they knew in their bones and blood that they were seeing home again.

Several of them rushed forward, but Olive stopped them.

"Wait!" she cried. "We have to pick the right tree. After all, it will hopefully be your home for hundreds of years."

So they walked all night and looked and perused and picked very carefully. And if you absolutely swear not to bother them and leave your camera at home, I'll tell you how to find the new home of the Algonquin brownies.

When you walk in through the Columbus Circle entrance of Central Park, follow the path to the left. Walk north for about ten or fifteen minutes until you reach Strawberry Fields. And there, deep in this part of the park, is a fine, grand oak (the third one from the right).

If you want to make sure it's the right one, look closely at the roots: you'll see that the brownies have inscribed a beautiful *A* somewhere in the bark, to honor the memory of an Algonquin that no longer exists.

I'm fairly sure that you'll want to know what happened to Olive.

She has moved with her father and the cat into another New York City hotel and is perfectly happy. In fact, she is now the city's youngest pastry chef, specializing in fruit pastries— which is quite an accomplishment. But I can't tell you which hotel; Olive is quite shy and very protective about her history with the brownies, and I must respect her privacy.

Mathilde, on the other hand, is ready to tell the story of the brownies to anyone who will listen. If you see a fat orange cat spread out across the concierge counter of a certain old-fashioned New York City hotel, you've likely happened across Olive's new home.

Fairies and Flowers

You've just learned about how important trees are to certain breeds of fairies. Many fairies are also intricately connected with flowers and flora in general.

Each type of flower has a secret meaning to fairies, so be careful about what flowers you put in a vase in your room or plant in your garden. Here's a short list of common flowers and what they symbolize in the fairy realm:

Carnations: friendship
Freesia: sweetness
Lavender: cooperation
Lilies of the valley: eternal youth
Peonies: indifference
Roses: truth, honesty
Tiger lilies: lies, aggression
Violets: celebration

Tulips symbolize loyalty, and a little bouquet of them on the kitchen table will do wonders in terms of making local fairies like you. Fairies cherish loyalty, which is one of the reasons they like dogs, the most faithful of animals.

Certain flowers are not flowers at all but are fairy creatures disguised by spells. The names of these blooms are surprisingly obvious: snapdragons and birds-of-paradise. The snapdragons do indeed become fairy dragons: their petals turn into scales and their stems become long green poisonous tails. Birds-of-paradise are beautiful to behold, either as flowers or fairy birds—but make sure to cover your ears if you see them in creature form: their song is shrill and terrible and sometimes causes a seven-year deafness.

Snapdragon   Bird-of-Paradise

Marigolds are important to fairies. At night, they wring the juice from the little petals on the underside of the flower into tiny glass jars and use that marigold extract for medicines and perfumes. Many gardeners today use marigolds everywhere from tennis clubs to store parking lots in the summer, since they're so hardy when it comes to the hot sun. If you look beneath a marigold plant and see lots of twisted loose petals, it's likely that fairies visited there recently.

Poison ivy leaves are home to the tiniest known species of fairy—practically microscopic—called the Maledendrom fairies. Each poison ivy leaf can contain as many as a thousand Maledendrom

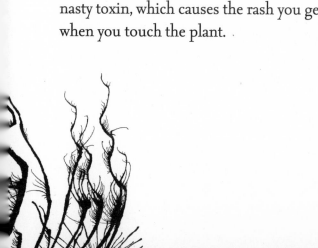

fairies, which hang upside down from hooked feet and wait for clueless campers and other victims. Their dartlike fingers are filled with a nasty toxin, which causes the rash you get when you touch the plant.

A Special Note
to Those with Gardens

If your family has a garden in your backyard, you would be wise to make some sort of welcoming gesture to the local fairies.

Take ten little rocks and make a circle near the garden's entrance, or on its left side if the garden has no gate. This is a universal sign to fairies that they can help themselves to growing vegetables and flowers.

In return, they will often ensure that your plants bear the sweetest tomatoes, the plumpest raspberries, or the most brilliantly colored hydrangeas. This practice has been used by knowledgeable farmers and gardeners for centuries.

Some gardeners leave dishes of salt nestled in the dirt to kill snails and slugs. The salt instantly dissolves these creatures; some humans even take pleasure in pouring the salt right on top of them. I strongly advise against doing this, since many fairies detest this cruel practice and will take offense. The result will surely be shrunken, hard green beans, uprooted turnips, rotten potatoes, and so on.

On another note, fairies love scarecrows. They think they're hilarious.

Why You Should Watch Your Step
on Baseball Fields,
Soccer Fields, and Other Vast Lawns

Be careful to stick to smooth, shorn parts of the grass, or you may have the misfortune of accidentally stepping on an enchanted tuft of grass that casts a nasty spell when trod upon.

Emerald-colored and stubbornly resistant to the blades of lawn mowers, these "Stray Sods" are relatively easy to spot. They are also impossible to uproot, and if you dig around the plants in the dirt, their fire-red roots retract from human sight, squirming like worms as they go. Fairies invented Stray Sods and use the milk from their roots for medicines.

People who stomp on a common Stray Sod are doomed to walk in circles for hours. As you can imagine, this would not be especially helpful if you stepped on one while playing a game of soccer, football, or baseball.

Other, more exotic breeds of Stray Sods contain highly specific spells that make you forget your name, or what year it is, or the word for "rain" or "snow" or "milk," and so on. These tend to be reddish in color and should be avoided at all costs, as the effects of the spells are permanent. Children who trod on the name-forgetting Stray Sod used to have to wear iron bracelets bearing their names until the end of their days.

Old Irish manuals advise you to wear your coat inside out when walking in fields, which apparently protects you against these odd spells. So next time you are playing ball in a field, it might be a good idea to turn your uniform shirt inside out—or wear an inside-out shirt under the uniform at the very least.

As you will see in the next story, Stray Sods and poison ivy fairies are not the only dangerous "flower fairies."

Setting the Record Straight About Ringing Bluebells

People have long believed that if you hear bluebell flowers "ring" like real bells, you are actually hearing your own death knell. In Scotland, the nickname for bluebells is "dead man's bells."

This is not true. If you hear ringing bluebells, it means that a fairy funeral is taking place nearby.

If you hear lilies of the valley chiming, on the other hand, you are near a fairy wedding.

Lily   Daisy   Rose   Violet

Tale No. 2
A Face Made from Flowers

When something has been unfair for a very long time, you'd think that someone would sort it out. But some unfair things never get sorted out: wars still happen all the time; storms ruin crops and sometimes even cities; some people live shorter lives than they ought to.

Another unfair thing that's been happening forever: in every family, some siblings seem to get all the lucky breaks, while another gets left in the cold.

That's definitely how it was in Daisy's family: her three undeserving older sisters were pretty, and Daisy was not. Like Daisy, her sisters had all been named after flowers—Rose, Lily, and Violet—and they looked as though they'd all been shaken from the same flower-seed packet and teased up from the soil of a sunny garden.

Daisy, on the other hand, might have been clipped from a hemlock patch: she was quite peculiar-looking, with a high moon of a forehead and an elegant arched nose that belonged on someone much older. Her ears stuck out, as though they didn't want to miss a single whisper.

Her mother never forgave her for falling short of her winsome name, and her sisters made fun of her.

"Your new name is Velma," they informed Daisy at breakfast one morning.

Daisy, who was eight, just stared at them.

"Don't you want to know why?" asked Rose. "Because 'Daisy' is too pretty for you. We stayed up late last night to come up with a name that would fit you better. So from now on, you'll answer to 'Velma' around here."

And later, the letters V-E-L-M-A appeared in pink nail polish on Daisy's bedroom door. Even after three coats of white paint, a hint of that insulting combination of letters remained.

I'm sure that you will rush to say, "Well, those sisters sound like nasty pieces of work, and they certainly prove that pretty isn't everything," and I would absolutely agree with you. But Daisy's family did not think the qualities that made Daisy special (sweetness, inquisitiveness, imagination) counted for very much.

But the beastly sisters did not know about Daisy's most extraordinary quality, which was, as you probably guessed, her fairy sight. Even so, the family knew that something was different about her, and the strangeness that always powdered the air around Daisy made her even less popular. Fairy sight makes you act very odd sometimes, when you're constantly seeing things that normal people are not. People might catch you talking to a fairy and think you're talking to yourself, or they might see you wearing your socks inside out all the time (for reasons you learned about in "How to Protect Yourself from a Dangerous Fairy").

Here's an example of Daisy's strange behavior: sometimes her mother would wake up to strange noises in the middle of the night. She would stumble out onto the upstairs foyer and squint through her cold-creamed eyes and see Daisy's shadowy shape creeping down the stairs.

"Where do you think you're going?" her mother would yell, and Daisy's little shoulders would clench up and she'd scamper back into her room. But one night, Daisy's mother didn't hear the stairs creak and by chance looked out the bathroom window at three in the morning and saw her youngest daughter sitting alone in the backyard of their Brooklyn house.

An explanation was insisted upon as Daisy was hauled back up to her room.

"I was sitting in the fairy ring," Daisy said at last, after ten minutes of stubborn silence.

"What are you talking about?" demanded her mother, and when Daisy pointed out the window at a round patch of

very green grass in the backyard, her mother scowled even harder.

"That's just where the table was last summer, which shaded the grass below and made it greener," she snapped.

"It's a fairy ring," insisted Daisy. She climbed onto her bed and buried her face in her pillow and refused to say another word.

Her mother stared at her. "Why do you have to act so odd all the time? Where did I go wrong?"

But these are questions that no little girl should ever have to answer; Daisy didn't even try, and so her mother turned out the light and left her daughter alone in the moonlight.

Later that week, in art class, Daisy and her classmates were given an easy assignment: create a picture of an object that you find beautiful. Paint jars and brushes were handed out, the scrape of brushstrokes and hum of concentration filled the room, and then it was time for show-and-tell. One of the girls held up a picture of her horse. A picture of a beach at sunset followed.

Then it was Daisy's turn.

"What is that?" someone shouted out.

"It's a flower fairy," explained Daisy.

"It's horrible-looking," said one girl. "Its hair and arms are made of thorny vines. Fairies are supposed to be pretty."

Daisy studied her picture and frowned. "This is a special kind, one that lives in fairy rings. I think it's beautiful."

The bell rang. The art teacher stopped Daisy on the way out.

"I think your picture is beautiful too," she told Daisy. "There are many different kinds of beauty in the world. Some beauty is very unusual and can even be scary. Most people don't understand that."

Daisy looked at her picture for a moment and then rolled it up.

"I'm tired of everyone thinking that I'm strange," she said. "Things would be easier if I was plain-pretty like my sisters."

"That's probably true," sighed the teacher, who remembered Rose and Lily and Violet from her old classes. "But you don't want to be like them. It's always better to be beautiful in a unique way. You'll appreciate that when you're older."

Daisy's eyes showed that her thoughts had drifted elsewhere.

"I think I'd like to be a flower," she said after a minute. "Or even a whole garden. Everyone thinks they're pretty. No one hates flowers."

The teacher smiled gently and smoothed down Daisy's hair. "No," she said. "No one hates flowers. Even the late-blooming ones."

Later that night, Daisy took the rolled-up picture out from under the bed, where she'd hidden it from her sisters. She looked at it for a long time. When she was done looking, she tiptoed down the stairs and then outside in her nightgown. The sky was black and moonless and it was very hard to see. Daisy glanced back at the house, but no sour midnight faces appeared in the windows.

She sat in the dark green patch of grass where the table had been last summer and waited.

Now, if you had been sitting next to Daisy in the dark, it

might have struck you as odd, how the grass began to fill with little glimmers of gold light. You might have thought that lightning bugs had nestled between the fat emerald blades, until you remembered that lightning bugs hover in the air and do not cluster by the hundreds in the grass. And then you would have to shield your eyes as the glimmer grew brighter and rose into the air until it wasn't dark at all anymore, but was instead brighter than heaven at high noon.

That's how it had been for Daisy the first time she sat in the fairy ring in her backyard; for a moment when all of that gold light came, she'd thought that she'd died and that angels were coming.

But angels did not come.

What *did* come with all the light would have frightened most children, but Daisy wasn't scared.

Vines began to stem from the ground. Soon you could see that these vines weren't vines at all. They were creatures that resembled tiny, grotesque humans, with thorn-covered, vinelike arms and legs and hair, and glowing luna-moth wings unfurling from their backs. Dozens of them emerged from the earth, and with silent industry, they went about setting up their nightly feast.

I probably don't have to tell you that active fairy rings are difficult to come by in the modern world. And just what these rings *are*, exactly, has long been the subject of much debate. Some believe that they mark the site of an underground fairy court or realm. Others think the rings are fairy graveyards.

The ring in Daisy's Brooklyn backyard just happened to belong to an extremely rare type of winged fairy, thought to be extinct until Daisy's story first got pieced together by today's fairy scholars, myself included. First seen in ancient times, these creatures were known in Greek as *anthothirios* (or "flower beasts") and in Latin as *Circaea lutetiana* (or "enchanter's nightshade"), due to their vinelike appearance and the fact that they only appear at night. Both the Greeks and the Romans wrote about the dangerous spells weaved by these creatures.

Such "flower beasts" are not mentioned in fairy literature again until the late 1500s. I came across the diary of an early Dutch explorer named Henry van der Hoots, who spent quite a bit of time with Native Americans in the area that eventually became Brooklyn.

Look at this curious entry written by van der Hoots on August 15, 1598:

> Tonight the Indians told me about a circle of land, not far from their camp, where they upon occasion see a "midnight shine" that rises like flames from the ground. During the day, the site of the "shine" is only a round patch of dark grass, about six feet in diameter. The Indians call it a place of dark spirits and claim

that several years ago an Indian child who wandered into the midnight shine disappeared like dust on the wind.

These Native Americans called the tiny, leafy creatures that scuttled about near the circle "midnight-shine spirits."

But in honor of the only little girl to see these "midnight-shine" fairies in centuries, I shall refer to them henceforth by Daisy's simple name: flower fairies.

⌘ ⌘ ⌘

Daisy watched the fairy feast in quiet fascination.

They ate terrible things like roasted ants and grasshoppers, and afterward they danced. If she moved, the fairies would stop abruptly and gaze at her and then resume their festivities, but they never invited her to join in. This lucky-and-unlucky girl never sensed that her situation was really quite perilous. As you will soon see, the ancient Greeks and Romans knew what they were talking about when they deemed this species dangerous.

But the flower fairies themselves never gave Daisy any hint of malice, and being near them soothed her, because she understood what it felt like to be considered ugly and odd and because they accepted her as she was and let her bathe in the gold light of their world. She thought about her sadness and wondered how to make it go away.

On this particular evening, the golden light in the fairy

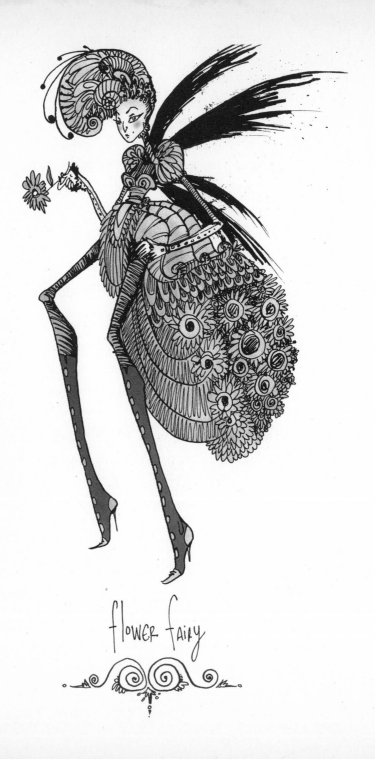

flower fairy

ring was brighter than usual and the flower fairies danced more beautifully than ever, and as she watched them, Daisy suddenly had an idea. A grim and gorgeous idea, and she made this idea into a simple plan.

She put the plan into action the very next day.

⚜ ⚜ ⚜

Have you ever noticed that all hardware stores smell the same? You can go into a hardware store in Lonely Hill, Alabama, and it will smell the same as one in Topeka, Kansas, or the one on Hudson Street in New York City. That afternoon, after school, Daisy ambled into her neighborhood hardware store, which smelled of the usual utility and determination and plaster and paint.

57

A man with red eyes and a bushy handlebar mustache peered down at her from behind the counter.

"What'll it be, half-pint?"

"I'd like to buy some seeds, please," said Daisy politely. "For flowers."

The watercolored seed packets were almost as pretty as any flower could be, and since Daisy wanted them all, she stayed for an hour making difficult choices. The hardware-store man gave her a brown paper bag, and when Daisy left, that bag contained seeds for sweet peas, foxgloves, meadowsweet, lady's slippers, and snowdrops.

Her sisters pounced when Daisy walked through the front door.

"What's in the bag, Velma," Lily hollered, trying to snatch it away from Daisy. But instead of going limp as usual, Daisy elbowed her way free and ran up the stairs, the brown paper bag hugged to her chest.

"I'm going to make something," she shouted back down at their mean little plain-pretty faces. "Something too beautiful for you to understand."

And she ran into her bedroom and locked the door.

Daisy turned the packets over and over again in her hands and she read the printed Latin names of each to herself until they became a strange, dead-language spell in her mind:

Galanthus nivalis,
Digitalis,
Arum dracunculus,
Spiraea ulmaria,
Lathyrus odoratus,
Cypripedium calceolus!

It was time for Daisy to plant her garden. She shook the packets out onto her white pillowcase.

And one by one, she ate every seed.

⊶ ⊶ ⊶

A strange spell indeed, those seeds cast. And a long-lasting one too: they held Daisy in a bright, frightening dream for days, vines unfurling in her mind, flowers blooming and rising until they were bowed by the sky. And then, suddenly, the spell was over: Daisy was in her bed and a circle of angry faces hovered over her.

"She's awake," someone said, and then her mother's face loomed closest.

"What were you *thinking?*" the woman cried. "Why did you eat all those seeds?"

Daisy's throat felt like sandpaper.

"Am I a flower?" she whispered.

"What?"

"A garden," murmured Daisy. "I'm a strange and beautiful garden. Do you think I'm pretty now?"

"She's still delirious," someone said.

"Crazy, more like it," said someone else. "Call the doctor again."

"*Galanthus nivalis,*" Daisy mumbled, and she fell back asleep.

~ ~ ~

It didn't work, Daisy's plan: she did not become a rich, strange garden; she did not turn into a beautiful flower; her family did not find her beautiful at last; in fact, they were wary of her now and she felt more alone than ever.

She stayed in bed for days and listened to all the normal-day sounds in the rooms around and beneath her: the clink of dishes; the opening and closing of doors; footsteps on the stairs, quieter as they passed in front of her door. And the whole time, Daisy thought about the fairy ring and the flower fairies and longed to visit it again. Had the fairies missed her? Did they wonder what had happened? On the seventh day,

Daisy's legs no longer wobbled, and that night, when the house and everyone in it were asleep, she crept down the stairs.

It was late October then; the ground was cold and the grass was starting to wither, even in the fairy ring. Daisy wrapped her nightgown tight around her body and hugged her knees to her chest as she sat on the lawn. A dog barked down the street; the wind blew dry leaves across the yard. For a moment Daisy's heart wilted in despair; maybe the flower fairies would not come tonight, or ever again. They were failing her when she needed to see them most.

But soon the gold light came and the vines unfurled from the ground; the fairy ring came to life, and the flower fairies appeared and began to set out their feast. Daisy spoke to them for the first time. She said simply, "Please make me beautiful."

The flower fairies stopped and stared at her, and this time they did not go back to their feast and their dances. They formed a circle around Daisy, and suddenly Daisy began to change. She grew smaller and smaller until her shoulders were even with the blades of browning grass and the sky drew further away. Her last thought was that maybe they were turning her into a thorn-covered flower fairy like themselves, which would be easy for her, really, since she already knew what it was like to be strange and alarming and secretive.

But the flower fairies did not change Daisy into a fairy.

They changed her into a flower instead, a frail little bloom, which basked each day in the weakening autumn sunshine until winter's first frost came and put the world to sleep.

There are two ways to look at this story. On one hand, it is possible that the flower fairies thought they were fulfilling Daisy's deepest wish by turning her into a flower, which would make this tale one of bittersweet, eerie loveliness.

However, as you now know, flower fairies have long been regarded as a darker species, and history suggests that their intentions were probably not so kind.

For thousands of years, people who have stumbled into fairy realms—whether through fairy rings or otherwise—have had spells cast on them. It's very likely that the first time Daisy entered her backyard fairy ring, the flower fairies used an enchantment to give her the seemingly harmless idea about becoming a flower in the first place.

And with each of her nighttime visits, they probably strengthened the spell to tighten their hold on her, and the simple idea gradually turned into something more dangerous. Once Daisy went so far as to swallow the seeds, the flower fairies had the girl completely in their power and took the final step to make her part of their "strange and beautiful garden" forever.

It's impossible to know for certain.

Further Notes on Fairy Rings

Over the years, many people have tried to remove fairy rings from their properties, but such a feat is impossible. No matter how hard you try to dig one up, it will always reappear, and the fairies that live there will make your life a misery.

If there is a telltale dark ring of grass in your yard, steer clear of it and touch it as little as possible. Fairy ring grass can be cut along with the rest of the lawn, but *never* dig into it, even if you think you're making a nice gesture by planting flowers there. It will be seen as a hostile gesture.

Over the years, many fairy rings have been unwittingly paved over to make roads (and there are always more car accidents at these points than at others) or partially dug up and filled in with the cement foundations of a house or business (no restaurant built on top of a fairy ring will ever succeed; meat rots, milk spoils, and bread molds faster at such an establishment than at the one next door).

One sign that your house is built on top of a fairy ring: ivy or some other vine grows with unusual quickness around the house, as though threatening to swallow it up.

Or: if hot water runs out quickly. This is because fairies in the realm beneath the house will take their share of hot water from the boiler first and leave the house's occupants to fend for themselves.

Another sign: animals like to crawl under the house or under the porch. Dogs, squirrels, possums, even skunks: all species are naturally drawn to fairy rings and like to lie on top of them. Fairies love most animals (see "Fairies and Animals") and pamper them when they visit.

If you suspect that your house indeed resides on top of a ring, there are certain things you can do to make the fairies less resentful. For starters, plant a fragrant rosebush at the southwest corner of the house; fairies especially like white cabbage roses. Or leave a bowl of flour on your back porch; fairies will borrow from it in the night.

It should be noted that not all fairy rings belong to the darker types of fairies, like the flower fairies we met in Daisy's tale. Fairy rings can also be sites of great joy, especially on spring and summer evenings. Old books mention spectacular fairy celebrations taking place on May Day, which a few privileged humans have been permitted to attend.

One ancient manuscript says that if you run around a fairy ring seven times at midnight during a full moon, you will be allowed a brief glimpse of the fairies even if you do not have fairy sight—although this doesn't work for most people. This is just as well, as fairies might think that you were spying on them.

The Link Between Fairies
and Diamonds

Like flowers, jewels are another important symbol of beauty. Diamonds are the most precious gems on earth. They are very hard to find, especially big ones, and they are extremely expensive.

But what people today don't know is that the diamond's glinting sparkle is actually a fairy soul.

The bigger the diamond, the more important the fairy was when he or she was alive.

Pink and yellow diamonds—the most rare—contain the souls of fairy royals.

If you hold a diamond up in the sunlight at high noon on May Day, look at its reflection on the ground and you may be able to see the outline of the fairy whose soul is inside.

As you will learn in the next tale, fairies are often connected with jewels in other mysterious ways as well.

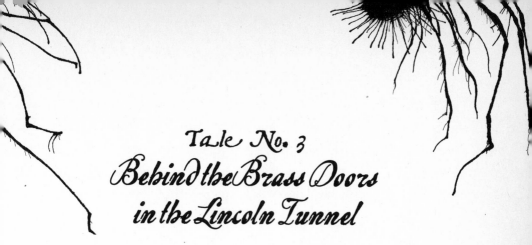

Tale No. 3
Behind the Brass Doors
in the Lincoln Tunnel

George was nine years old when he learned that his parents didn't know everything. It was an unsettling revelation, and this is how it happened:

They were in the car, driving out to the Jersey shore for a summer weekend away. George's parents sat up front while George sat in the back with the family's dog, an Irish setter named Pretzel. Pretzel, of course, did not resemble a pretzel at all, but that's neither here nor there. The car was stuck in traffic in the middle of the Lincoln Tunnel.

Now, I don't know if you've ever had the pleasure of riding through the Lincoln Tunnel, which runs under the river between New York City and New Jersey. It's a stinky, grimly lit affair, with walls the color of old coffee-stained diner mugs. I'm fairly certain that President Lincoln, for whom the tunnel is named, would have picked something else to honor his memory, but he just got unlucky in this respect.

Anyway, there are two good things about the Lincoln

Tunnel, from a child's point of view. The first is the big, fat blue line painted down the tunnel's walls at the exact center, where New York becomes New Jersey and vice versa. It is always fun to stick your hand as far as you can into the front seat, toward the windshield, so you can officially be the first in the car to cross over the line.

This is what George was doing at the moment.

"Hey, knock it off," snapped his father, who was driving. He batted George's hand away.

"You're distracting your father," said George's mother. "Sit back and put your seat belt on."

George flounced back in his seat and crossed his arms over his chest.

"I didn't hear that seat belt click," said his mother.

George put on his seat belt and stared out the window at the second interesting thing about the Lincoln Tunnel: the small brass doors that stood about every hundred feet or so. They looked strange to George, like bright gold teeth in an old yellowing smile.

"What's behind those doors?" he asked.

"Oh, just pipes and stuff," said his father distractedly. "Gears. That sort of thing."

Pretzel leaped across the seat and landed on George's lap. He barked at the window, steaming up the glass with his dog breath.

"What's he barking at?" George's father frowned, peering in the rearview mirror.

George shoved Pretzel back to the other side of the car and looked out the window.

"Hey," he said. "He's barking at that weird little man with the really gross beard."

George's mother craned her neck around to see what he was talking about. "What weird little man?" she demanded.

"That one," George exclaimed, and indeed, a very small, very weird man stood next to one of the brass doors. A gray matted beard gushed from his chin and dragged on the dirty tunnel floor; flies buzzed around it, and George thought he saw some sort of half-eaten sandwich nestled in the middle. A red pointy hat teetered on the man's crown.

"Where?"

"Right there," shouted
George, pointing, and Pretzel bounded into
his lap again.

"It's like a zoo in here," wailed George's mother, reaching over the seat and pushing the dog down onto the floor. She stared at George. "I suppose you think you're being funny, making up a story like that."

George looked out the window again. A cobwebby gray cape covered in pockets hung from the man's shoulders, and he rooted around in these pockets until he fished out a big, rusty key. And just liked that, he opened one of the little doors with the key and disappeared inside, the door slamming behind him.

"I'm not making it up," George said crossly. "He just went in through one of those doors. You're just too old and slow to see him."

This, of course, did not go over very well; the shouting from both parents in the front seat sounded like this: "What! How dare you! Lie! Sass your mother! Shame! That's enough! Too old to tell lies! Fib! Not another word!"

And at that exact moment, George's world tilted slightly and it did not tilt back to its old spot again—not that afternoon, or ever again. Because he knew that he was right and his parents were not, that there *had* been an ugly little man with a smelly beard and a rusty key, and it had suddenly become clear that adults didn't know everything about everything after all. George still felt weird until they stopped for gas on the other side of the Lincoln Tunnel but very nearly forgot about it when ice cream came onto the scene shortly thereafter.

The following week: School. Homework. Soccer practice. George's mother served an especially nasty meat loaf on Wednesday night that should probably remain undescribed. In other words, a normal week.

But then, that weekend:

"Mom! Dad! That man is there again—look!"

George and his family were stuck in traffic again, just past the fat blue halfway-point line down the middle of the Lincoln Tunnel.

"Pipe down back there," said his father, squinting out the front windshield.

"We're never going to get there," complained George's mother, ignoring her son.

Well, it is *very* hard for a boy of nine to resist a lightning-does-strike-twice mystery dangled a mere two feet from him. The little man was very real and as dirty as ever, although the sandwich appeared to have fallen out of his matted beard (or, George reasoned, it had been discovered and devoured as a midnight snack). He opened the same little brass door with his key and disappeared inside. Just as the door was about to close, George leaped out of the car and stopped the door with his sneaker.

It was strangely silent on the other side of that door, and George found himself at the beginning of a corridor, a very dark one with a low ceiling—a tunnel within a tunnel. The dirty-bearded man must have picked up a flashlight or a lantern, because a dim light shone far down the tunnel, and as that light got farther away, a black-ink darkness seeped into the air around George. Not wanting the yellow flicker to disappear and leave him in that bog of black, George hurried down the cramped tunnel.

The tunnel bent left and right and then left again, and George could hear the little man hack and cough in the dark ahead. George's hair filled with dirt from the tunnel ceiling, and it got in his eyes too. He was just wondering if anyone else had ever followed the man down this secret passageway deep below the Hudson River when the ground suddenly curved sharply downward and George was sliding down—

first head over heels and then heels over head—until . . . *ooph!*

He was in a deep pile of leaves.

The fall knocked the breath out of him and he lay there stunned until the air filtered into his chest. Gulping deep leaf-dusted breaths, George realized that it was light again. He burrowed through the pile and peered out the side.

It was an impossible sight, but there it was: an endless, dimly lit forest of trees with black-green leaves and thick, ropy trunks; blood-red fruit dangled from the branches.

Mist swirled around the gnarled roots of the trees like a snake. A harvest was happening, an under-river harvest of

that ripe, strange fruit, with hundreds of little bearded men working in the trees. The sound of chimes filled the air, and George noticed tiny silver bells tied to each tree branch that tinkled every time a man reached up and plucked a piece of fruit.

Several of the little men stumped over to the leaf pile where George hid; they started to chat in deep, crabby, rasping voices that reminded George of a garbage disposal grinding up a fork.

Then the first little man wedged a dirty, stubby finger up his nose and dug around with great gusto.

The second one began to burp: deep, satisfied, thunder-crackle belches. George found this very entertaining.

And then, for good measure, the third man added to the conversation by bending over and letting out a great crackling fart. The discussion got louder and so did all of the accompanying noises until there was a symphony of grunts, burps, and, well, you know.

This probably shouldn't have been the first hint that these little men were not human grown-ups, who, as we all know, never pick their noses or burp or any such thing.

In fact, these men were dwarves.

I'm sure that you've at least heard of dwarves. Of all the fairy species, dwarves most closely resemble humans and are often considered less magical as a result. Under certain circumstances, this can be a dangerous misconception, because dwarves are just as handy with spells as the next type of fairy.

But in general, they are not malicious creatures. This is mostly because they dwell underground and inside hills and mountains and don't usually bother with the world of people. In fact, they have terrible eyesight from dwelling in such lightless places and often have to rely on their sense of smell to get by. Throughout history, dwarves have been known as miners and great metalsmiths, although there are, of course, some varieties of dwarves who have nothing to do with fire and shovels and melders.

The Harvester dwarves of the Lincoln Tunnel are a perfect example; they were much handier with gardening shears than picks and axes. Another reason that Harvesters are black sheep within the dwarf family is that they spend a considerable amount of time in the human world, as you'll see shortly.

And here's the funny thing: this breed is famous for copying the most repulsive habits of men, which, as you've seen, range from nose picking to burping to much worse behaviors. Not that the dwarves know these habits are rude; they just see people doing them all the time and therefore probably think that they are casual, appropriate behaviors.

There have been sightings of these ill-mannered Harvester dwarves all over the world, but they're believed to be indigenous to Spain, southern France, and Italy. I find them very amusing and was delighted at first to hear that they'd cropped up in New York City—that is, until I heard the outcome of this particular tale.

No matter how funny these gross little "men" might appear, remember that the same rules apply to dwarves that apply to all fairies. Keep your distance, never eat their food, and never, ever steal from them.

If only young George had stuck to these guidelines.

Let's hasten back to George's story.

⚙⚙⚙

The downside of being a witness to this burp-and-fart-filled conversation soon became clear: George had to pinch his nose shut and breathe through his mouth. And just when he thought he would never breathe clean air again and that the dwarves would never go back to their harvest, they grabbed the edge of the fruit basket and dragged it away.

Cherries, thought George as he squinted at the fruit inside, but there was something odd about these cherries, the way they sounded in the basket. They sort of *clack-clack-clacked*, as though they were made out of glass.

Another dwarf struggled past George's leaf pile with a full basket, and every few steps, his beard tangled with his feet and the basket lurched to one side, spilling cherries onto the mossy ground. George reached out from the leaf pile and grabbed one.

He turned it from side to side.

It was not a cherry.

It was a *ruby*.

The nose-picking, smelly dwarves of the Lincoln Tunnel were harvesting rubies.

Thousands of them, maybe even millions. And the one in George's hand was a very big one, the size of a walnut, maybe even bigger.

And just looking at it made George think about grabbing a bunch of them, a sack if he could, a sack of pirate loot. And then he started thinking about how famous that big, fat sack of glistening, juicy rubies would make him. George, owner of the most mysterious and wondrous rubies the world had ever known. George, the richest boy on the planet. He could buy whatever he wanted. His parents would have to ask him for an allowance instead of the other way around. It would be too wonderful.

He reached out of the leaf pile and groped around on the ground for the rest of the fallen rubies and shoveled them into his shorts pockets. Then he rolled some up in his socks. But this wasn't enough. George surveyed the scene from his roost. It would be hard to steal more: there were practically as many dwarves as there were rubies, and they didn't look exactly friendly.

And that's when he saw it.

Glinting, swaying gently, twisting lazily around on its stem: the biggest ruby of all, a big red apple of a ruby. And George suddenly wanted it more than he'd ever wanted anything in his whole life.

Just then, a whistle blew across the forest, a strange melancholy sound like a ship in a foggy nighttime harbor.

All of the little men climbed down from the trees and yawned and stretched their arms. The silver bells stilled as the dwarves lay down and spread their dirty beards over their bellies like blankets.

Within a few seconds, they all fell asleep.

The only thing that dared to move in that under-river forest was the fat, ridiculous ruby: it rocked smugly on its branch.

George climbed out of the leaf pile and tiptoed past the snoring dwarves. Their sleep was a deep opium sleep: thousands of snores rumbled across the forest floor. Not one dwarf stirred as George crept along—not a flicker of an eye or a missed breath.

A ladder leaned against the fat ruby's tree, and George quietly propped it up against the fat ruby's branch. Up the rungs, quietly, carefully, knees wobbling a little from fear; then the fat ruby was within an arm's length—and then George's hand was just beneath it.

He plucked the ruby from the branch.

The little silver bell tied to the branch began to ring. George grabbed at it, but then the bells on the other branches started to chime. The chimes spread to the next tree, and then the next, and the one behind that, and soon every silver bell in the whole forest rang as though a five-alarm fire was happening.

George panicked and fell off the ladder. His arm made a sickening *crunch* and his hand went limp and out rolled the fat ruby; it looked very happy and satisfied to have been the cause of such a ruckus.

The dwarves suddenly opened their eyes and sat up as straight as chairs; a thousand fingers went into a thousand noses and suddenly George was being pelted with boogers as he grabbed the ruby and ran. By the time he reached the rabbit-hole tunnel, a revolting, gummy dwarf-booger crust covered George from head to toe.

Why aren't any of them following me? he thought as he climbed back into the hole, a very painful process when one has a very broken arm.

Behind him, the tree bells rang more violently than ever, a storm of angry chimes; yet no footsteps followed George and no angry faces appeared in the entrance to the tunnel. George staggered up the dark tunnel hill and groped his way back along the walls.

I'm getting away with it, he thought jubilantly.

The booger-covered fat ruby glowed and nestled in the crook of his good arm like a puppy.

George's shorts pockets suddenly felt heavier. At first George thought his imagination was playing a badly timed trick, but quickly he realized that his imagination wasn't doing anything at all and that the rubies actually were weighing him down, trying to root him to the ground and trap him in the tunnel.

Maybe the dwarves weren't letting him get away after all.

George unzipped his ruby-filled shorts and ran down the tunnel in his underwear. But then the rubies in his rolled-up boogery socks started acting up, growing heavy as croquet balls and then bowling balls and then anvils, until George could hardly lift his legs anymore. He took off his shoes and peeled off the socks and the rubies thudded to the floor. The dirt from the floor and ceiling stuck to the boogers all over his body.

A rectangular outline of fluorescent light shone in the dark ahead: the edges of the brass door leading back to the Lincoln Tunnel.

George began to run again, miserably expecting his prized ruby to clatter heavily to the ground. But instead the fat ruby nuzzled him and stayed curiously warm, strangely buoyant; it practically *hummed* to itself. George reached the rectangle of light and yanked the door open.

And there it was at last: real life, the real world—in all of its yellowed-tiled and exhaust-filled glory.

The door clattered shut behind him and horns honked angrily as George stumbled into the tunnel. The flash of red and blue lights nearly blinded him: a dozen police cars were parked around George's car—which hadn't budged an inch since he'd disappeared into the ruby forest.

George's parents stood outside their car, clinging to each other.

"He just disappeared," his mother sobbed. "We turned around and he was gone."

"I'm right here!" George shouted, still gripping his prize, and he ran toward the car. Pretzel barked wildly when he saw him.

The policemen turned around.

"Get out of here," said one of them, shoving him.

"Ow!" George yelled, pain shooting through his broken arm. "Are you crazy? I'm their kid! They're looking for *me*! Mom! Dad!"

George's parents looked over at him and their hostile, empty faces stopped George in his tracks. Then his mother's face crumpled and she sobbed again. The policeman stepped forward again.

"I said *beat* it, you filthy, crazy old bum," he hissed, raising his baton. "That's a fine prank to play on a lady who's just lost her son. If you're not out of here in ten seconds, we'll haul you down to the station as a kidnapping suspect."

George was stunned. Old *bum*?

Then he caught a glimpse of himself in a car window and his heart nearly stopped.

Half an hour earlier, George had been nine years old. But according to that car window, now he was a gnarled old man, covered in dirt and grime, with a grungy tangle of hair and a matted beard and long fingernails.

He began to scream.

A few minutes later, he was in the back of a police car, cold handcuffs tight around his bony, still booger-covered wrists. The rearview mirror confirmed that George was still a dreadful old man, and he trembled with shock.

Then he realized that the ruby was no longer warming his hand. It had shrunk and turned cold.

George unfurled his fingers.

The fat ruby was gone.

In its place lay a scab-covered dead mouse.

As my mother used to say: nothing good ever comes to those who steal, and that's doubly true when it comes to stealing from fairies.

∞ ∞ ∞

After hearing about George's woeful tale, I set out to investigate this strange operation under the Hudson River myself. Through a little detective work, I learned that every Friday afternoon, one of the dwarves would take some of the harvested river rubies into the city to sell to a jewelry dealer named Mr. Gary Weinshank, a tall man with icy blue eyes and wild, curling white eyebrows. This dwarf would remain invisible to human eyes until he emerged from the tunnel and then cast a spell to make himself appear human while he did his weekly errand. Mr. Weinshank knew this strange little man as Peter C. Movaat.

Well, if you rearrange the letters in that name, you get the following Latin phrase:

CAVEAT EMPTOR

... which means "let the buyer beware."

George had spotted this Mr. Movaat returning from two such business trips, and the boy's fairy sight allowed him to see through the dwarf's disguise.

And that vile booger crust had transformed George into an old man on his trip back through the dwarves' secret tunnel.

The exact door that led George to the ruby forest has been sealed up long ago, no doubt by the Harvesters themselves. Mr. Weinshank claims that Mr. Movaat recently disappeared and that they no longer have business dealings together, although I suspect that Mr. Weinshank is simply protecting his lucrative source of rubies. The Harvester dwarves of the Lincoln Tunnel must still be there, under the river, growing fat rubies and selling them in the real world.

But until I can locate the new door to their fantastical little kingdom, I cannot prove it.

The Difference Between Dwarves and Trolls

It's no surprise that these two species are often confused: both are generally short and gnarled and ugly, and associated with underground habitats.

Dwarves get very sniffy when mistaken for trolls, and who can blame them? For the most part, dwarves are industrious, harmless creatures (unless they are harassed or stolen from), whereas trolls are *always* up to no good. They are professional ne'er-do-wells.

Dwarf

If you come across a dwarf or troll-like creature and can't figure out which one it is, here's a good rule of thumb: if your encounter takes place near a bridge, you've likely met a troll. That's where they usually make their homes; they sit around underneath their bridge of choice and complain about overhead traffic, drafts, and graffiti. Trolls happen to be terrific complainers and grumblers.

But if you happen to be near a mountain or a hill or someplace with an underground passage, like a tunnel, the creature is likely a dwarf, since—as you know—dwarves mine or harvest in these areas.

I cannot emphasize enough how dangerous trolls can be: they weave strong spells and are well-known thieves and kidnappers. Worst of all: sometimes they eat children. The lucky few who manage to escape the clutches of trolls often hear voices for the rest of their lives or are plagued by a tiredness so heavy that they cannot get out of bed.

troll

If you live near a bridge and suspect the presence of trolls, there are certain precautions you can take. Carry a mirror with you at all times. Trolls hate seeing their reflections; it depresses them to see how ugly they are. They'll go well out of their way to avoid a mirror.

Not many people know this, but if you take a bite of peanut butter before you cross a bridge, no troll will ever bother you. They detest the smell of it. It absolutely nauseates them.

One further note: don't leave your dogs tethered outside alone for long periods. While trolls may despise humans, they love dogs and won't hesitate to take yours as a pet.

Money in the Fairy World

Every fairy breed has its own currency.

Amusingly, one branch of the brownie family uses coffee beans as money, and so they're very happy that there are Starbucks and other coffee shops on practically every city and town corner these days.

Goblins barter fruits; blood oranges, star fruit, and pome-granates are worth the most, while regular apples and bananas are like pennies and nickels.

Trolls use animal bones; the bigger the animal, the more the bone is worth, and they especially prize femurs. These nasty creatures often make midnight runs to their "banks": the garbage bins behind butcher shops—and graveyards. You should be warned that trolls value the bones of children above all.

As you've just seen in Tale No. 3, dwarves deal in cold, hard cash, since they occasionally have secret business dealings with humans.

On that note, fairies have actually extensively influenced how human money has been made and used over the centuries. For example, many years ago, east coast Native Americans used a thick white shell called wampum as money. What most people don't know: wampum was introduced to the tribes by the Wampum fairies, who cast spells on the shells to edge them with bright splashes of purple. The fairies traded these magically altered shells to the natives for corn silk and other harvested goods, and soon the native tribes began to trade the shells among themselves.

Did you ever wonder why American dollar bills are green? Long ago, a rural tribe of fairies used mint leaves as money, which gave one of their human neighbors (who just *happened* to be an important designer of America's paper money) the idea to make paper bills out of a pale green paper.

One last note: don't forget that money in America is made at the U.S. Mint. See the connection?

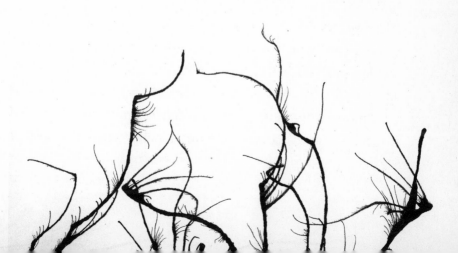

Why You Shouldn't Trust Fairy Godmothers

In people's minds, money and fame often go together. I'm sure that you've heard many times about so-called fairy godmothers, who drift about, granting wishes to humans who crave both treasure and acclaim.

Such happiness-spreading creatures are nonsense, although one diabolical type of fairy likes to take advantage of the human tendency to always wish for what one doesn't have. Known as the Crone fairies, this repulsive, wizened tribe of female-only creatures can literally smell human yearning from up to five miles away. When approaching her victim, the Crone casts a spell to make herself appear as a silver-tressed, beautiful old woman with kind eyes and a soft mouth.

The Crone approaches the human and offers to grant a wish. She then tells the person to place his hand in hers as he makes the wish. Now things get ugly. The moment a human touches a Crone's hand, that person's wish is granted instead to his worst enemy. So, if a young boy wishes to become rich and famous, suddenly his rival will land a record deal or some such, leaving the boy on the sidelines to watch helplessly.

An important note: the Crone fairies tend to hang around magazine stands, since the Crones believe that the sort of people who read tons of magazines tend to have very big (and often unrealistic) dreams. So be on guard around such venues.

Incidentally, neither money nor wishes can buy fame; only talent, hard work, and a little bit of luck will make you famous. And in any case, as you will see in the next tale, the unrelenting quest for fame can have some very nasty results.

Tale No. 4
Unlikely Performances at Carnegie Hall

This story is about one of my favorite fairy breeds: the Librettos.

"Libretto" is a musical term, and the winged Libretto fairies are indeed very linked to music. In fact, they dwell inside musical instruments (especially those made of wood, since, as you now know, many fairies have strong associations with trees); the disposition of the fairy that lives inside a violin determines whether its music sounds sweet or shrill.

A libretto is simply a book containing words of an opera. The minuscule Libretto fairies got this curious name because they often hide inside books of music. Entirely black-and-white, they camouflage themselves by rolling up and hiding in the dots of musical notes on paper, fooling even the most astute fairy spotters like myself.

Libretto fairies cannot abide bad music; in fact, they often appoint themselves guardians of musical standards, even though no one ever officially asks for their opinion. So, if you are a flute player or some such and you just happen to blow a bad note around them—*watch out*. Librettos specialize in sharp little pinches, and sometimes they do far worse things, as you'll soon see. You'll rarely find them in schools, since they simply cannot stand the sound of an amateur orchestra—but a Libretto colony lives in nearly every major concert hall around the world.

Libretto

Which brings us to the setting of this story: Carnegie Hall, a fine, venerable concert hall that has stood on West 57th Street in Midtown Manhattan for more than a hundred years.

One autumn evening, about a year ago, Carnegie Hall was being prepared for a piano concert of great importance.

Workers rushed about, dusting off lightbulbs, swiping the seats with stiff-bristled brushes, neatening stacks of paper programs. A magnificent black grand piano was wheeled out onto the stage, where it gleamed under the spotlights like a highly polished gun. Microphones were tapped, and the nervous stage manager straightened his bow tie over and over again.

Baba Hudu was about to arrive.

Don't tell me you've never heard of Baba Hudu! He is only one of the most famous pianists in the world, and he has quite a distinctive look. A very heavy beard and mustache run wild across the bottom of his face, and a thick carpet of black hair springs from the crown of his head. This is between you and me, but frankly I never understood how Baba Hudu's hair stays so dark and bushy; after all, he must be about four hundred years old by now.

Here's an interesting fact about Baba Hudu: he always looks so bored when he plays that sometimes you wonder if he's actually dead and find yourself peering up into the stage's ceiling to see if long strings are operating his arms. But he's not dead at all; he actually is as bored as he looks. After all, he considers himself to be the long-reigning master of his instrument, with nary a tune or a composer left in the world to challenge him, and audiences are just lucky to pay to hear him play. Or so he thinks.

Carnegie Hall's population of Libretto fairies did not feel the same way.

While many instruments are played in Carnegie Hall, the Libretto fairies live inside the enormous piano that had been wheeled onto the stage for the concert. They remembered Baba Hudu's last concert, the previous spring: those heavy eyes, that weary look, those meaty arms that he could barely be bothered to lift to the keyboard. He had plunked out a

Beethoven concerto and then oiled his way off the stage, not even bothering to stay for applause.

This time, however, the Libretto fairies planned to treat the audience to a rather different sort of Baba Hudu performance.

The lobby lights lowered and rose again: it was eight o'clock, time for the concert to begin. The audience sat down and waited eagerly. Fifteen minutes later, Baba Hudu meandered out onto the stage, tolerated some clapping, and took his seat on the piano bench.

The orchestra began to play.

Baba Hudu closed his eyes and his body swayed slightly, as though he was asleep on a gently rocking train. He brought his hands down onto the keyboard. And then, just as he began to play, he let out a terrific scream and shot up off the bench.

The audience gasped. The conductor waved his baton, struggling to keep the orchestra in tempo.

Baba Hudu composed himself, brushed off the front of his suit, and sat down again. He began to play.

A quiet, lovely part of the concerto came along, and Baba Hudu's eyelids grew heavy again; his chins quivered with stately authority. He had just begun to play the sweetest part of the lullaby when suddenly he jolted up again and let out another girlish hoot. The orchestra members looked at each other in disbelief as they played on. The audience snickered and giggled.

Angry now, Baba Hudu pounded out the next part of the concerto. What had been a lovely lullaby now sounded like a military march. As he thundered to a finish, the lid of the piano suddenly slammed down, barely missing Baba Hudu's sausage-y fingers.

If that wasn't enough, Baba Hudu's famous black hair flew right up off his head—as though it had been caught by a fishing rod and yanked away. The stage lights gleamed on Baba's perfectly bald head as his toupee magically danced in mid-air above the orchestra.

Then it fell to the stage—front and center, right where Baba Hudu should have been taking his bow—and lay there in an insulting, hairy puddle.

Needless to say, the Baba Hudu debacle came to be regarded as one of Carnegie Hall's most adored performances.

The Libretto fairies cherished the embar-rassment of Baba

Hudu. Inside their piano, they celebrated their coup for days.

But when a fireworks show is over, there is always a long dark night afterward; the giddiness of the Baba Hudu victory did not last long.

And now we get to the main part of our story.

I've often seen one identical twin finish the other's sentence and vice versa. It shouldn't be a surprise: after all, everyone knows that identical twins are essentially one person split in two. And yet it's still always a shock to see such telepathy at work.

The case of Mirabelle and Annabelle Destinatus has astounded many people. Eleven years old, identical in every way, the Destinatus twins were already the most famous piano duo in the world. Mirabelle and Annabelle played in spectacular, unfathomable harmony and received standing ovations at concerts in every world capital; their matching red velvet dresses crisp and perfect and taut as paper, their black Mary Jane shoes shining under the spotlights, a single pearl on a lacy silver chain nestled in the hollow of each of their throats. They looked like Christmas cookies, like sweet holly berries, like angels, even; they were adored and complimented and coddled.

"The Yin and Yang of Perfection," sighed one newspaper headline.

"The Destinatus Twins Are the Eighth Wonder of the World!" exclaimed another.

Perhaps you're seeing through these girls already, even if they managed to fool everyone else. Mirabelle and Annabelle were most certainly not Christmas angels; behind the facade, they were dreadful little attention-craving beasts. Spiders and strategy filled their thoughts, and battery acid gurgled in their shameless hearts—even though their fingers spun air into shimmering golden music.

And here's the unfair thing: the Destinatus Duo was on the verge of becoming more famous and adored than ever.

They were about to make their first appearance at Carnegie Hall.

Several days before the big debut, the twins arrived at the hall for a practice session. The Libretto fairies found their home being wheeled out on the stage for Mirabelle; another gleaming Steinway was fetched from storage for Annabelle.

Annabelle glared at the storage piano and then at Mirabelle. "I want your piano," she said.

"Too bad," said Mirabelle, running her fingers tauntingly along the sleek curve of the Libretto fairy piano.

"You always get the better piano," snapped Annabelle.

"That's because I'm the better player," said Mirabelle.

Annabelle marched up to the Libretto fairies' piano and gave it a swift kick. "A donkey's a better player than you," she said.

Mirabelle's face grew red. "Well, a pig's a better player than you," she informed her sister, and swiftly kicked Annabelle's piano, leaving an ugly white scuff on the paint.

Then Annabelle grabbed a Coca-Cola from a shocked

worker at the side of the stage and dumped it inside the Libretto fairies' piano.

Several fights exploded at once: between the twins, who rolled on the floor and scratched and kicked each other, sending shreds of velvety red dress into the air, and another between the duo's manager and the owner of Carnegie Hall, who in the end only agreed to let the Destinatus twins play because so many tickets had already been sold.

It took three German piano specialists—flown in from Berlin at the last minute—to repair the cola-drenched piano. As the specialists worked, the twins—friends again—smirked in the wings. After all, they were the Eighth Wonder of the World.

They could get away with anything.

❦ ❦ ❦

You have learned by now how attached fairies become to their homes and how vengeful they can be when those homes are threatened or defaced in any way. And the Destinatus Duo had made the Libretto fairies' beautiful Steinway piano unlivable for days—and had almost ruined it for good.

When the German workers were finished—the day of the big debut—the enraged Librettos convened on the keyboard to discuss an appropriate punishment for the twins. They agreed that it must make the humiliation of Baba Hudu pale in comparison.

Suddenly a shadow darkened the keyboard; the Libretto fairies looked up to see two sets of ice-angel eyes staring down at them.

"They're so tiny," said Mirabelle, squinting at the fairies. "I've never seen such tiny fairies, have you, Annabelle?"

"Like little fleas," replied Annabelle. "Just like those fairies at—"

"—Royal Albert Hall in London," said Mirabelle. "We sure taught them a thing or two." She poked at one of the Librettos, who rewarded her with a sharp bite on the fingertip.

"Ouch!" she cried, snatching her finger away. A nasty smile lifted the corners of her red mouth. "Should we—"

"—teach them a lesson too?" Annabelle interrupted. "Yes, we should."

Then both twins sprang toward the keyboard and began to thunder out a wild Prokofiev duet.

The lucky Librettos flew away just in time; the unlucky ones got quite bashed around by this attack of pinkies and thumbs and all of the fingers in between. When the twins finished pounding out the piece, they stalked around the hall, hunting the bruised Librettos—who had slipped through a gap in the floorboards and reconvened under the stage.

"We know where you ar-r-r-re," Mirabelle called, and the girls took turns spitting through the slats of the floor.

It was five o'clock then. The concert was at eight.

The Librettos had only three hours to plan their vengeance on the rottenest girls who'd ever crossed a fairy's path.

Eight o'clock: the lobby lights raised and lowered. Ushers closed and guarded the concert hall doors against annoying latecomers. Two pianos shone on the stage, facing each other, their curves hugging like sleek black creatures in an embrace. Clad in velvet, Mirabelle and Annabelle glided out onto the stage; the audience burst into applause.

"Aren't they *darling?*" cried one woman to her friend.

"Like china dolls," gushed the friend. "Adorable."

Silence fell over the great hall as the Destinatus twins sat

down at their pianos. Across the expanse of wire strings and wood and hammers, they gazed deeply into each other's eyes.

Without so much as a nod, they began to play at the exact same moment.

"They're absolutely reading each other's minds," exclaimed an awestruck woman, but everyone was too transfixed to shush her. No one had ever seen anything like it. The twins appeared to be in a trance; never looking at the keys or their music, Annabelle and Mirabelle stared only at each other and played in perfect tandem.

In fact, they didn't even seem to notice the Libretto fairies climbing up the sides of their piano benches.

First came the pinches, which had worked so nicely on poor Baba Hudu, and the fairies made those pinches extra hard this time—guaranteed bruise-leavers—with lots of hard little twists.

Neither of the twins even blinked.

The Librettos were baffled. They pinched even harder, on the soft white undersides of the girls' arms and the warm backs of their necks—and didn't even get a twitch in response.

Mirabelle and Annabelle had been scratching and pinching and tormenting each other for so many years that they had grown completely impervious to pain.

The Librettos switched tactics.

They crawled onto the music sheets propped up in front of each twin, rolled themselves up to resemble black little dots, made a wild mess of the notes on the scores—and gleefully waited for the sour notes to come.

Those bad notes never came.

The Destinatus twins were playing their entire performance from memory. And then, at the exact same second, the twins swatted the unneeded music sheets to the floor.

It was time for drastic action. The Libretto fairies began to chant.

Slowly, the pianos began to turn away from each other, as though by magic, breaking the twins' concentrated gaze. Annabelle and Mirabelle didn't miss a beat; they simply stood up and played on the pianos as the instruments swung around the stage. The astonished audience clapped right in the middle of the performance, more impressed than ever.

"It's like a magic show and concert all rolled up into one!" shouted an old man, growing almost too excited to remain in his seat.

The twins finished their piece in perfect unison and, flushed with triumph, ran to the center of the stage. The audience stood up and shouts of "Bravo! Bravo!" filled the room. Annabelle and Mirabelle curtsied again and again.

Just then, the twins looked down. A young Libretto fairy—a baby, really—lay on the floor, still dazed from its fall with the music sheets. The girls looked at each other and nodded. Annabelle lifted her shiny Mary Jane shoe and brought it down, right on top of the fairy.

Squelch.

The lights flickered and dulled and suddenly the hall went black. The audience gasped. Then a single spotlight beamed down on the stage, drenching the Destinatus Duo in a harsh, blinding white light. The girls squinted and covered their eyes. Not knowing what to do, the audience began to clap again.

Suddenly the twins put their hands over their ears and began to scream, their faces screwed up in great pain. Tears streamed down their cheeks—and just like that, Mirabelle and Annabelle ran off the stage.

The Destinatus Duo has never performed in public again.

Even the sweetest puppy will act like a dangerous wolf if provoked. The Librettos usually reserve their magic for practical jokes. But like all fairy breeds, they can wield powerful spells. When Annabelle cruelly killed one of their ilk, the fairies used the strongest one at their disposal:

A curse that turns a person's greatest desire into a nightmare.

What did Mirabelle and Annabelle crave most in the whole world?

Adulation. Adoration. Applause.

But after the Librettos finished with the girls, applause no longer sounded like clapping. It sounded instead like the most awful noises in the world: bombs falling, women screaming, babies crying from hunger, fingernails on chalkboards—and that's just the beginning.

It's a shame, in a way, because the girls really were quite talented. But since their debut at Carnegie Hall, they have only played for each other, sequestered and nervous, without praise or compliments—and far away from the glow of any stage.

Fairies can *always* see what you really are. Take note.

Music and Fairies

Music plays a very important role in the lives of all fairy breeds, not just the Librettos. The earliest recorded fairy sightings describe great fairy feasts with wild dancing and raucous music, not unlike the celebrations Daisy saw in her backyard fairy ring.

Music played by fairies may sound odd to human ears; at the very least, it often sounds nothing like what we consider "music." Some people who have returned from fairy realms (and survived to tell the tale) describe it as "shrill" or "rhythmless" or even "horrid"; yet others recall it being the "most beautiful sound" they've ever heard.

Fairy instruments range from the very simple to the extremely complicated; some are provided by nature: a seashell used as a horn or a rolled-up leaf made into a trumpet. Yet most are highly wrought handmade inventions that defy explanation, and the noises they emit are unlike any we hear in our daily lives. One child rescued from a fairy ring said that her fairy captors played a lullaby to make her drowsy. When asked to liken the sound to one in the human world, the little girl said it was sort of like the lowing of great whales; it was a "terribly lonely sound."

Dwarves often play something akin to gigantic organs

deep within their mountain lairs; the powerful reverberations from the organ pipes are often mistaken for earthquakes by humans on the outside, and dwarves' performances have been known to wake up even the sleepiest volcanoes.

Be careful when listening to fairy music: while it can be the treat of a lifetime, like fairy food, sometimes it is used to cast irreversible enchantments over humans. If you find yourself at a fairy concert and your eyesight begins to dim or you feel any numbness in your hands or feet, put your fingers in your ears immediately. These are signs that the music is putting you into the fairies' power.

Many fairy breeds are great appreciators of human music. In eras past, they have been particularly drawn to certain instruments rarely played today, such as the lute. If you play the guitar, which is distantly related to the lute, a hidden audience just might be listening to you practice.

Fairies in Your Kitchen

In the fairy world, music and food always go hand in hand. Fairies love feasts and food, but most of them hate to cook for themselves, as you'll see in the next tale. They *can* do it, of course, but once in a while, they like to help themselves to humans' cupboards. It's sort of like going out to dinner at a restaurant or shopping in a supermarket—except it's free.

The following commonplace items are very popular:

- Oatmeal or any cereal made from oats (a staple of their diets)
- Vividly colored fruits, such as ruby-red grapefruits, blood oranges, lemons, blueberries, and blackberries (the fairies drain the colors and use them as dyes for fairy cloths and other fabrics)
- Cornflakes (a very popular snack)
- Whole milk or cream (used for bathing)
- Pretzel sticks with salt (I'm told that they hang them up like salamis in their kitchens and shear off the salt as needed)

They also adore these more exotic but still findable items:

- Lemongrass (which they tear apart and weave into blankets)
- Flaxseed (used to make breakfast cakes)

- Poppy seeds (widely eaten, but also used to make beaded necklaces)
- Crystallized ginger (the ultimate fairy delicacy, served at fairy courts)
- Pomegranates (used in large fairy feasts, with each fairy getting one plump seed)

Fairies like trinkets that resemble animals, making gummi bears, animal crackers, and goldfish crackers popular. They also enjoy cereals like Lucky Charms and will steal all of the colored marshmallows from the box.

They sometimes take Velveeta cheese too; they *never* eat it but instead use the rubbery substance as a building material.

Here's a short list of human foods that fairies *hate*:

- Skim milk (they think thinned milk is a sacrilege)
- Gorgonzola cheese (they abhor the stink of it)
- Peanut butter (trolls are not the only ones with an aversion to it—who knows why?)
- Vinegar (imagine being a tiny creature and getting a strong whiff of vinegar)
- Pepper, especially white pepper (most breeds are wildly allergic to it)

It's best to hide these items in the back of your cupboards or refrigerator.

Incidentally, cakes never fall in the oven on their own accord; fairies take great pleasure in stomping on them when no one is looking. It's the joke that never gets tired.

I'm sure that you've heard the old saying "A watched pot never boils." Indeed, humans do seem to get extremely impatient while waiting for water to boil; fairies know this and it amuses them to throw ice into heating pots of water while your back is turned. This of course slows the amount of time it takes for the water to boil, and if the mischievous fairies are lucky, they may be treated to a tantrum on the part of the watching-and-waiting person.

On the Temptation of Spoons

This may seem random, but while we're on the topic of kitchens, I thought it was worth bringing up.

For some reason, fairies simply cannot help themselves when it comes to stealing spoons; they take them all the time. Teaspoons appear to be great favorites, although no variety of spoon—soupspoons, serving spoons, slatted spoons—is safe from a fairy.

To protect your silver spoons from going missing, tie them together with a piece of red ribbon or red string; this will ward fairies off.

If you open your cutlery drawer and a silver knife is missing, don't be alarmed. Fairies have probably borrowed it to carve a roast at a big feast. It will be returned within 24 hours; fairies believe that it's bad luck to keep a human's knife, and they're probably right.

However, most things that fairies "borrow" from humans are never returned, as you'll see in the next story.

Tale No. 5
The Number One Train

Felix liked having a name with an *x* in it; people always remembered it. This would come in handy later in life, when he was a rock star—which he had planned on becoming since he was about, say, three years old.

I'm sure that many people want to be rock stars but don't really do anything about becoming one, but Felix, who was now twelve, was not one of those people. In his opinion, the best rock stars played the guitar, and so three times a week after school, he went for a guitar lesson way downtown at the Greenwich House Music School with a man who was so good at the guitar that he could play it behind his head *and* with his toes.

Felix always took the subway downtown, the number one train, and one afternoon, while he stood on the platform with his guitar case, he looked down on the tracks and noticed a big, fat rat lumping along.

Usually subway rats scurried away as quickly as their rodenty little legs would carry them, but this fatso took his time, carefully inspecting the ground and not caring at all if anyone spotted him from above. Eventually he seemed to find what he was looking for: a pair of broken spectacles. The rat picked them up with his long yellow teeth, lumbered back into the dark train tunnel, and disappeared. Felix found this odd, but soon the guitar chords to Led Zeppelin's "Stairway to Heaven" became a more pressing matter and he forgot all about it.

But then, the following Thursday: there was the fat rat again; this time he sniffed around the tracks until he found a hat that had fallen off some unlucky man's head, a once-handsome fedora with a pheasant-feather band. The rat picked it up and tossed it onto his back; soon it looked like a hat with legs was waddling away into the tunnel. Felix laughed and glanced around at the other people standing on the platform, but no one else had noticed this comical sight.

From then on, Felix saw the rat every time he stood on the number one train's platform. The creature always retrieved strange items: a dirty glove, a holey sock, a boot (which was quite an ordeal to drag into the tunnel), a dirty red mitten, a tennis shoe with green laces. Watching the rodent carry away a filthy scarf printed with yellow smiley faces one afternoon, Felix wondered what kind of odd nest the animal was building.

He didn't have to wait long to find out.

It became hot for May; one afternoon a heat wave cooked the city in hundred-degree heat. Felix waited on the subway platform and fanned himself with his sheet music. Usually several other people stood around, waiting for the number one train, but today the platform was empty. The train seemed reluctant to arrive. Felix sat on a bench, took out his guitar, and began to strum a quiet song.

A cold rush of air gusted over him and Felix looked up to see if he was sitting under an air-conditioning vent, and that's when he saw it:

An odd figure standing at the far end of the platform, near the tunnel.

Felix blinked. The person certainly hadn't been there a moment earlier, but nor had he come down the stairs from the street, which were on the opposite end of the station.

The figure walked toward him now, wearing peculiar attire for a hot afternoon: a long, tattered overcoat with the collar up, a dirty hat, mismatched gloves. Two completely different shoes gave the figure a lopsided gait. A pair of glasses glinted on a face hidden behind a scarf, and Felix almost laughed at the awful outfit until he saw that the scarf had smiley faces on it and remembered that the rat had taken a smiley-face scarf into the tunnel weeks earlier. Then he realized that the figure must live in the tunnel with the rats and he stopped laughing.

Suddenly the figure stood in front of Felix and Felix found himself putting his guitar in its case. The figure pointed with a red-mitten-covered hand toward the tunnel and then Felix was following him into that dark subway tunnel—guitar in hand—walking on the iron rails. The light from the station faded away.

They took a right turn and then there was dirt under
their feet instead of iron rails. Felix didn't know how long he
walked and he couldn't even see the figure in front of him. All
he knew was that his heart was pounding and he couldn't stop
walking or turn around; a strange spell seemed to be pulling
him along, like a big magnet attracting a paper clip. Felix
couldn't even shout for someone to come and save him; that
same weird spell had shrunk his voice down to a pale little
mouse squeak.

A door opened in front of them, spilling a dull yellow
light into the black air, and then Felix was in a long hallway,
still clutching his guitar.

Several fat rats gathered around the figure's feet; they
whisked away its hat, overcoat, shoes, smiley-face scarf, red
mitten, and glasses—leaving the figure clad only in a hooded
cloak with very long sleeves. Folds of fabric hid the man's face
completely, which scared Felix more than a pair of glowing
red eyes or some such.

Another door opened on the far end of the hallway and
a second cloaked figure floated in, and then another, and
another.

Soon the room was full of them.

Felix found himself trapped in a den of goblins, deep in
the tunnel of the number one train.

Goblins are nasty, silent creatures with very ugly little faces. Usually they're quite small, no taller than a toddler, but these days some breeds in the Western Hemisphere grow as tall as human adults. They dwell in underground lairs and labyrinths, modeled after rat mazes.

When appearing in human realms, goblins often take the shapes of animals like cats or owls, or else they shroud themselves entirely in human clothes to hide their horrid appearances. They are incurable thieves and kidnappers, and also great "tempters," meaning that they offer up enchanted fruits to humans that will put them under the goblins' power— or worse, kill them. As one famous poet once wrote:

> We must not look at goblin men,
> We must not buy their fruits:
> Who knows upon what soil they fed
> Their hungry, thirsty roots?

While goblins have a very bad reputation, they're actually rather boring when it comes to their day-to-day lives. They're as lazy and slow-moving as slugs; Felix must have felt as though he'd traveled for miles through that subway tunnel, but in reality they'd only gone several hundred yards before entering into the goblins' lair. One of the main reasons goblins kidnap kids in the first place is to make them do much-hated housework and chores—and provide entertainment.

And on that note, let's get back to poor Felix.

The goblins watched Felix silently. Or at least Felix felt that they were watching him, but he couldn't tell for sure because of those sinister, face-hiding hoods. One goblin raised his right arm, and Felix felt his eyes closing.

When he opened his eyes again, he found himself in a room with several other children his age. A boy stood over him, staring into Felix's face.

"Who are you?" he demanded.

"I'm Felix," said Felix. "Who are you?"

"I'm Dick," said the boy. "Well, Richard, if you want to be formal about it. I'm named after the president."

"The president of what?" asked Felix, confused.

"The United States, dummy," said Dick. "Don't you even know who Richard Nixon is?"

Felix stared at Dick. Now that he got a good look at the boy, Felix realized that Dick's clothes looked, well, wrong somehow. His tight button-down shirt had big flowers splashed all over it, and his yellow pants swung like bells around his calves and ankles.

"Nixon hasn't been president for a million years," Felix informed him. "And you look like you belong on The Brady Bunch or something in those clothes."

"Aw, man," said Dick, slumping against the wall. "I'm never gonna get out of here. And if you think I've been here a long time, check her out." He pointed to a pale girl in the corner, who wore a floor-length calico dress, lace-up booties, and a bonnet. "That's Mary. She still thinks the president is someone named Theodore Roosevelt."

Felix sat up in disbelief. "What are you all doing here?" he asked Dick.

"We work for them," Dick said.

"Doing what?"

Dick   Helen   Flossie   Mary   Buster

"We each do different things," Dick told him. "I deliver messages and do errands around the lair. Mary was a baker's daughter in the real world, so she cooks for them. Buster builds things for them." Dick pointed to a scrappy-looking boy wearing a vest and newsboy cap. "And Helen and Flossie are their maids." He pointed at two girls in the most old-fashioned clothing of all: long pioneer dresses.

"I've never even *heard* of the guy who was president when *they* came down here," Dick added. "Some dude named Franklin Pierce." Then he looked at Felix's guitar. "I guess they brought you down here to play for them."

"Oh," managed Felix. "Really."

"Yeah, we thought that they might be going back out to get another kid," Dick continued. "When the rats started coming back with those clothes and glasses and things. That's when

we know one of the goblins is going to get dressed up like a person and go into the real world. The rats are their advance scouts. They probably had their beady little eyes on you for a while, you know."

"I saw them every day," said Felix, his throat dry. A rumbling noise shook the room and dirt fell loose from the ceiling.

"It's the subway," explained Dick. "Just overhead."

Felix could hardly believe it. "Wait, it's right *there?*" he exclaimed. "Don't you ever try to run away?"

"Sure," said Dick. "But it never works."

"Why not?"

"Try it and find out for yourself," whispered Dick. "But I'm warning you: the goblins never sleep, and they never leave a door unguarded. We've tried to dig tunnels out ourselves, but the rats always find out and squeal on us. You might as well get used to it here. There's no way home."

As it turned out, Dick had been right about the music. That evening, Mary was called away to prepare the goblins' supper feast; Helen and Flossie went with her to serve it. Dick and Buster went also to set up the chairs and table. Felix was left alone in the room until a small goblin brought Felix and his

guitar into a very long dirt-walled-and-ceilinged room. Fires roared in dug-out fireplaces.

Felix sat in an empty chair against a wall and waited.

Soon nearly a hundred cloaked goblins filed into the room in two lines and took their seats on either side of a long banquet table. Helen and Flossie carried in large bowls containing the first course. The food inside them looked like spaghetti to Felix and his stomach rumbled.

"Trust me, man, you don't want it," whispered Dick, who was standing next to Felix. "It's worm spaghetti."

Felix blanched.

"You're lying," he said to Dick.

"Night crawlers and maggots," Dick told him. "Mary has to cook whatever she can find in the ground. Wait until you see what comes next."

The second course looked like some sort of stew. Felix's stomach started to rumble again.

"Look closer," whispered Dick. Felix squinted at the stew pot as it was passed down the table and saw a boot bobbing about on top. And a broken wristwatch, and then a batch of unhappy-looking cockroaches.

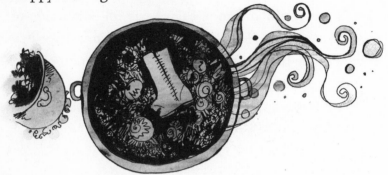

"A good rule of thumb: try to eat as little as possible around here," Dick told him.

"That won't be hard," Felix whispered back.

"Yeah, but not just because the food is gross," warned Dick. "You never know which food is enchanted and which food isn't. Enchanted food will put you in their power, and if you eat enough of it, you'll turn into one of them. There used to be a lot more of us kids, you know," and he nodded at several smaller cloaked figures at the end of the table.

Sweat began to pour from Felix's brow. Just then, the room fell silent and all hundred goblins turned around and faced him.

It was time for Felix to play his guitar.

His hands trembling, he pulled the guitar up onto his lap—and then his mind drew a blank. What on *earth* was he supposed to play for a roomful of subway-dwelling goblins?

Do something easy, he told himself, although his hands were so numb that he didn't know if he could manage anything at all.

The first song that came to mind was "Good Day Sunshine," by the Beatles.

He strummed his guitar and began to sing:

I need to laugh, and when the sun is out—

Suddenly all hundred goblins stood up angrily; the soup boot was violently hurled in Felix's direction, missing him by inches.

"Don't sing anything about the sun," hissed Dick. "They hate the sun. Do the worst, most boring song you can think of."

Felix faltered—until he remembered one of his lessons, when he and his ultra-cool guitar teacher had been messing around and making fun of a corny singer called Barry Manilow, who sported a fluffy bouffant. They would sing Manilow lyrics at the top of their lungs and howl with laughter as they played along.

Lady, take me high upon a hillside,
High up where the stallion meets the sky—

This one definitely counted as the worst song Felix could think of now, and so he started to play it.

The goblins sat back down and began to sway from side to side, obviously enjoying the music a great deal. It was just Felix's luck to fall captive to completely un-cool, Barry Manilow–loving goblins. When the song was over, the creatures stood up angrily again, which was Felix's cue to start from the beginning.

He had to play the song *twelve* times before the goblins let the children go back to their room.

Bed was a burlap sack stuffed with straw. Felix made himself wait until the other children were asleep before he would let tears roll down his cheeks.

⤜ ⤜ ⤜

At first, there was no way of telling time, and Felix began to wonder how long he'd been in the lair. A week or a decade? Who was president now? Who was on the cover of *Rolling Stone*? When the goblins came back with the next kid, would Felix himself look like he was wearing some period costume?

But then he figured out an easy way to keep track of the

days: every time a subway rumbled overhead, he knew that about twenty minutes had passed, and he began to keep an elaborate number-one-train schedule in his mind. Felix would imagine the people in those trains overhead, on their way to a boring day at work, or to a bowl of canned tomato soup at home, or to a new movie at a downtown theater, and this was how Felix stayed connected to the real world and kept his wits about him.

He began to look for ways out, but his hopes for escape waned quickly. Dick had been right: the goblins appeared to be everywhere. Sometimes when Felix would walk toward a door, a goblin would simply *appear* in front of it, out of thin air.

The rats ran loose everywhere too, carrying documents and other items around the maze for the goblins and spying on the children with their vicious little black eyes. Felix wondered how the other children had survived down there for so long, dwelling without hope.

But then something happened that showed Felix that hope springs eternal, even in the most seemingly resigned of hearts.

Mary rarely spoke; she kept her head down and her face expressionless as she made breakfast, lunch, tea, and supper for the goblins. She never grimaced as she dug up worms, or complained as she flattened roaches and coated them in dirt and fried them up.

One morning, the 5:02 subway rolled overheard as usual, and the wall torches lit themselves, as they did every morning. The children opened their eyes and stretched and yawned—and then they realized: Mary was gone.

Her plan had been ingenious, from what the children were able to piece together later that morning. For hygiene reasons, Mary's kitchen and her worm garden were the only places where the rats were not allowed to snoop; it turned out that she'd been digging a hidden tunnel for years from the worm garden. She'd dug a little bit at a time, using the discarded dirt in her recipes so there would never be a telltale pile to tip off the goblins.

Now the rats crowded into the worm garden, sniffing around, looking for the entrance to Mary's secret passage.

"Maybe we can find it first," Felix whispered to Dick, Helen, Flossie, and Buster, and for the first time, he saw a glimmer of excitement in their eyes.

"But it's gonna be harder than ever to walk around the lair now," said Dick, who as the messenger boy knew the maze better than anyone. "Both the goblins and the rats will be watching us closer than ever."

Just then, they heard a great chorus of rat squeals: a wild celebration had begun.

Mary had been brought back.

She had made it out of the lair; once on the subway tracks,

she'd nearly been flattened by a speeding train. She ran toward the yellow light of the station anyway, but peering up at the platform, Mary found that she was too terrified to venture into the alarming, electric modern world. That's where the rats found her—trembling on the verge of freedom—and before she could gather the courage for a leap up onto the platform, she had been whisked back to the goblin lair.

Everyone was summoned to the banquet room: all hundred goblins, the army of rats, and then the children.

A little goblin came into the hall, carrying a tray of beautiful red pomegranates, glistening with silvery water droplets. He set it down at Mary's feet.

Felix was confused.

"Why are they giving her such nice food?" he whispered to Dick. "I thought they'd want to punish her for running away."

But then Felix saw that Dick had tears in his eyes.

"They are punishing her," Dick whispered back, and he was right.

Mary had to eat all of the goblins' strange, luscious red goblins' fruit—and after that, she never uttered another word or tried to run away again.

಄಄ ಄಄ ಄಄

The lair fell back into its grim routine, and gradually Felix stopped keeping track of time. There was no point. The schedule in his mind became soft and faded, he stopped listening for the encouraging subway rumbles, and soon he even stopped noticing the dirt that dusted his neck each time a train went by.

Night after night, he played his guitar for the goblins— the same awful, tired Barry Manilow song—while the beasts swayed back and forth. Felix eventually stopped hearing the music and just played along numbly, waiting until they'd had enough and he could go to sleep.

Then one night, he had a strange, vivid dream. His guitar teacher was sitting in the lair with him.

"Dude, I can't believe you're playing Barry Manilow," the teacher scoffed to Felix.

Felix's face got red.

"Don't tell anyone," he begged.

"Whatever—I'm gonna tell *everyone*," said the teacher. "And what's more, don't come back to me for lessons when you get out of here. I don't want my cred to plummet because you've become such a loser."

Felix jolted awake, his heart pounding. It had been such an awful nightmare that he was glad to get back to his life in the goblin den.

But that night at supper, as he strummed his Barry Manilow tune for the millionth time, Felix got mad.

He knew that his destiny was to become a huge rock star, not some feeble dinner entertainment in the middle of nowhere.

How *dare* these goblins rob him of his greatness?

And with that, Felix narrowed his eyes and angrily strummed out the first lines of his old favorite song, "Stairway to Heaven."

He cringed and squeezed his eyes shut, waiting for the goblins to shoot out of their seats and throw things at him, or do something even worse.

But nothing happened.

In fact, there was not a sound in the room, besides the crackling fire. Felix opened his eyes. The goblins sat as still as statues, as though time had suddenly stopped. After a few seconds, they began to stir again, clearly not realizing that they'd been frozen, and they stared up at Felix expectantly.

Felix began to play the usual little Manilow recital, but his hands were no longer numb. In fact, his heart beat faster than it had for days, maybe weeks; blood flushed his cheeks. Once the goblins started swaying, Felix daringly switched to "Stairway" again—and the same thing happened.

The goblins froze.

This time, Felix kept playing and did not stop. Something about the tune was having a near-magical effect on his captors, and for the first time, he saw an opportunity to escape.

"Dick!" he shouted. "Look at them—now is our chance!"

Dick looked around the room nervously. "But what if they wake up?" he cried. "And what about the rats?"

"Throw the food to them!" yelled Buster from the far side of the room. "Now! You too!" he shouted at Helen and Flossie, and the children grabbed the bowls of wormy food from the table and threw it on the floor. Swarms of rats scampered over to the worm piles and began to devour them. Felix played "Stairway" furiously, hoping whatever spell he was weaving would hold up.

"Follow me!" shouted Dick. "Run!"

The children ran hard, leaving the famished rats and the frozen goblins behind, down through the dirt tunnels; the flames from the torches blazed to the ceilings, angry to see the children escape. Felix's guitar swung crazily on its neck strap and he tried to play as he ran to keep the spell going. They passed a room containing a crystal table, and on that table gleamed a tray of succulent red fruit—a deadly reminder that made the children's hearts pound even harder.

"That's the door out," cried Dick, and it was: beyond the door

there were no fire torches and it was black-dark as they staggered along, and soon they heard a sound, the most beautiful sound in the world:

The number one train was approaching.

They smashed themselves against the walls as the train tore past. And then when it had gone, the children ran toward the platform light and Felix almost cried when the newspaper stall—with its stale Baby Ruths and hard Snickers bars and magazines—came into sight. Helen and Flossie hustled along as well as they could in those long dresses, holding them up in front, showing the sort of lace pantaloons that young girls haven't worn since before the Civil War.

Felix threw his guitar onto the platform and heaved himself up, pulling Dick and Buster and Helen and Flossie up after him. The five children collapsed on the pavement, gasping for breath.

They were free.

"Where's Mary?" cried Helen suddenly.

Another number one train rumbled through the station and out again on the other side. Felix and Dick leaped down onto the track and stared into the tunnel. Had Mary followed them and fallen behind?

Just then, a quiet shape came toward them from the darkness.

"Let's get out of here," cried Dick. "What if it's one of them, coming to get us?"

"It's not," yelled Felix. "Look—it's Mary."

It *was* Mary, silent Mary, in her sweet calico dress and lace-up boots, standing there, still as a pale ghost in the black tunnel.

"Hurry up!" cried the children. "They'll be coming soon! Oh, please hurry."

But Mary just stood there and watched them sadly for a few minutes longer.

And then, without a word, she turned and disappeared back into the darkness.

There are clearly two lessons to be learned here. Firstly, once you have eaten goblin fruit, there is no way to save you. Never, ever taste a piece of it—or *any* fairy food, if you can avoid it— no matter how hungry you are or how delicious it looks.

And secondly, of all the fairy breeds, goblins are the most responsive to music. This is the only proven way to get the better of them. Some chords and melodies inexplicably freeze them, and Felix was lucky that—miraculously—"Stairway to Heaven" was one of them, for other melodies have been known to make goblins *more* powerful and even savage.

One tale tells of a lucky little girl who was able to bewitch some goblins who'd stolen her little sister: she played a frenzied sailor jig on her French horn, and, unable to control themselves, the goblins danced until they turned into a frothing stream of water. Unfortunately, this effective tune was never written down and saved for posterity; otherwise it would have served as a surefire way for any human to whistle his way out of goblin captivity.

Upon their return to the real world, Felix and the other children became known as the Subway Stowaways, and their case baffled the world. New York City records showed that two sisters named Helen and Florence "Flossie" Browne had gone missing in 1854, a Benjamin "Buster" Jenkins vanished in 1932, and a Richard "Dick" Murphy had disappeared in 1969.

And yet here they all were, real as night and day—and looking *exactly* the same as when they had vanished decades earlier. Scientists, astrologers, and even beauticians all clamored to know their secret, but of course no one believed their explanation.

However, there were no records of a missing girl fitting Mary's description, which was not unusual for a poor baker's daughter—probably an immigrant—in the early twentieth century. When the Subway Stowaway children insisted that the police go back into the tunnel to find her, they were unable to find an entrance to the "alleged goblins' lair" (as the newspapers called it), and no sixth child was ever recovered.

Time in the Fairy World

As we've just seen, time in the fairy world runs according to its own rules, and no human has ever figured out exactly what those rules are—not even me. Fairies have discovered how to manipulate time: speed it up, slow it down, stop it altogether when it suits them. If humans were to uncover time's secrets in this way, it would be considered the most important discovery in the history of our species, but right now that skill belongs exclusively to the fairies.

We have no way of judging the accurate age or life span of fairies; there's no rule of thumb, such as "One human year equals seven dog years"—although we do know all fairies eventually grow old and die, like humans.

Each breed appears to slow time at different stages in life according to varying priorities. For example, dwarves value wisdom and experience, and so they speed up their youths and remain wizened and elderly in appearance for most of their lifetimes. Many winged fairies—especially those associated with flowers—tend to favor youth and beauty and therefore "freeze" themselves at younger stages of life; they die suddenly, without wrinkles or any physical evidence of old age—but they age internally regardless, and their bodies just give out without any visible warnings.

As you now know, humans who wander into fairy realms are greatly affected by the strange behavior of time there. Some enter as adults and reemerge as babies; they find themselves speaking in backward sentences as time rapidly reverses itself. Some captives emerge from fairy realms after being there for decades and find themselves the same age as when they "disappeared," as you saw in Felix's tale.

And yet others—as you saw in George's tale—others enter the fairy world as children and come out old and decrepit. More than once, a human has come out of a fairy realm and simply turned to dust, the way that bodies do when they've been underground for a very long time.

Clocks often behave strangely around fairies, as you'll remember from the story about the Algonquin brownies. If you notice that your wristwatch has stopped or is just suddenly wrong altogether or if your grandfather clock chimes at odd hours, that may be the reason—a fairy may be nearby.

If you wake up feeling especially groggy, you may have slept longer than you thought: if a fairy had anything to do with it, you might have been dreaming for days or even weeks, even if your clock says that you were only asleep for eight hours.

End of the Free Ride

When you have to travel from point A to B, you simply get into a subway like Felix, or a car or a train or a plane, and off you go.

Fairies, on the other hand, have a much harder time traveling long distances, and astonishingly enough, the smaller varieties of fairy have traditionally traveled long distances by letter. That is, before you seal up an envelope containing a letter or note, they will crawl inside and simply hitch a ride.

But these days, who sends letters? The only envelopes that get sent out of our houses contain bill payments and other unpleasantries, and no fairy in its right mind wants to hitch a ride to a telephone company payment center.

Here's how you can turn this situation to your advantage: buy some nice paper and pens and start sending letters to your friends and family in different parts of the country—or to a faraway king or head of state. Why not send a letter to a famous author, intrepid reporter, or Hollywood star as well? Fairies will soon learn that your room is an outpost for adventurous letter travel, and they've been known to reward today's rare letter writers with gifts and strange, lovely dreams.

Garbage Dumps and Other Unlikely Fairy Habitats

Most winged fairies are great aesthetes, meaning that they love beauty. But a few breeds could care less about prettiness, and the modern world offers them plenty of tempting places to live, like the filthy subway goblin lair you've just visited.

Vast stinky garbage dumps and landfills provide excellent homes for gnomes, who are aboveground cousins of dwarves. Like dwarves, gnomes are squat creatures with huge, bulbous noses and absolutely filthy long beards. They dislike humans and scenic nature in equal parts, so today's sprawling, people-free, disgusting garbage dumps are the perfect place for them.

Dump-dwelling gnomes build hidden houses from discarded plywood and cinder blocks and furnish them with thrown-away refrigerators, couches, mattresses, and tables. Next time you walk past your local dump, take a close look at the heaps of trash. Do you notice anything odd, like smoke rising from them? If so, gnomes probably live there, in a house carefully hidden beneath piles of garbage, and are enjoying a fire in a makeshift fireplace. Or perhaps the smoke is coming from a gnome kitchen, where they are cooking a stew of banana peels, dirty diapers, rancid meat, and coffee grounds.

However, I certainly don't advise that you wade through the trash to find out.

Sewers make fine homes for goblins, while natural history museums are easy places to spot brownies. In New York City's Museum of Natural History, the famous dioramas of trees, bushes, and taxidermy animals are absolutely overrun by nature-starved brownies at night.

Laundromats are also great after-hour destinations for small fairies of all breeds; they love to take turns spinning in the dryers.

You would think that flower stores would be enticing fairy habitats, but they are not. Fairies get very attached to certain trees and other plants, and it upsets them when those plants are sold off and carted away.

Enchanted Fairy Isles

Now it's time to leave the garbage dumps behind and explore one of the more beautiful and fantastical kinds of fairy habitats: enchanted fairy isles.

Recorded sightings of enchanted fairy islands are very rare, but they exist in all four oceans, in each of the seven seas, and in countless rivers on six of the seven continents.

Some of the islands dwell underwater and silently rise to the surface on moonless nights; others are always above water and shrouded in fog—or are simply invisible to human eyes. No human has ever set foot on a fairy island—or if he has, he has not lived to tell us about it.

The most famous fairy island, Tír na nÓg, stands in an Irish lake, and savage battles are the favorite pastime of the fairies living there. They don't even care if they get wounded or killed, because on Tír na nÓg, those warrior fairies will simply come back to life the next day, their wounds healed, their bloodied axes clean again.

There are islands similar to Tír na nÓg in the United States, including one in the Mississippi River near St. Louis, and another in the Rio Grande, and yet another in the Yellowstone River.

There is even one in the East River, between Manhattan

and Queens. In fact, a river-spanning commuter cable car passes directly above it many times a day.

It's really quite extraordinary how many people zigzag over that nameless, invisible island each day, on their way to work or on their way home, thinking about things like television shows or electricity bills or turkey sandwiches on pumpernickel bread—oblivious to the wild fairy battles taking place a hundred yards beneath their feet.

Oceans and rivers and streams offer up all sorts of additional exciting fairy activity, as you will see in the next story.

Tale No. 6
The Ballad of Big Edd

In case you weren't aware, mermaids are also fairies—one of the few species that you don't need fairy sight to glimpse. There are many different kinds of them all around the world. I particularly like the Arctic mermaids, who build shimmering underwater ice palaces, an army of seals and walruses at their command. Equally fascinating are the terrifying Amazon River mermaids, often mistaken for enormous piranhas. Over the years, more river explorers have fallen prey to these creatures than to malaria or poison arrows.

But, of course, the most well known of the dangerous mermaid breeds is the Lorelei.

The term "the Lorelei" implies that there is only one, but there are actually hundreds of them, part of a large order ruled by a strict queen. Each one sits upon rocks in the middle of the sea, combing her long, golden hair. Sailors who spot a Lorelei and hear her bewitching songs are supposed to automatically fall under her spell; they usually crash their ships into the

rocks where the Lorelei perches. No one knows whether those men die or are kept as her slaves.

You probably think that the Lorelei are terribly wicked creatures, but I feel bad for them sometimes. They're quite sad, actually, and very lonely. Imagine sitting out there on a rock in the ocean, with absolutely nothing to do but steal sailors once in a blue moon, having no one to talk to or laugh with—not now, or ever.

To make matters worse, each Lorelei is assigned by the Lorelei queen to a different part of the world, with no consideration for that mermaid's individual happiness. She could end up shivering in the bitterly cold English Channel or coughing in the most polluted part of the Ganges River in India. Or off the coast of Alaska, where Lorelei are regularly harpooned by hunters in helicopters, who mistake them for some sort of harbor seal.

Or she could get assigned to the waters off the coast of . . . Staten Island.

And now we get to the main part of our story.

Imogene had a rather unusual life for an eleven-year-old girl. She lived on Staten Island (part of New York City just across the water from the Statue of Liberty) in a fragile glass greenhouse with her grandfather. They raised orchids in this greenhouse, and they slept and cooked and ate their meals in a little shack next to the glass building.

Every morning Imogene woke up at five, when the rest of the city was still heavy with sleep. Grandfather, with his shock of white hair, would be up already, sitting in the greenhouse, drinking coffee and reading the newspaper, his fingernails black with rich soil. Imogene too would drink a cup of coffee and eat a piece of bread and jam and listen to the newspaper pages turn and the sound of warm drops of water falling from the greenhouse's glass ceiling; she would breathe in the faint, silken scent of the flowers and watch the stars disappear overhead one by one, until the last bite of bread and jam was gone.

Then it was time to tend to the orchids.

She and Grandfather would move silently up and down the rows of flowers, waking them up, tickling their faces, watering them. Then the sun would rise over the greenhouse, revealing a sea of pale yellows and violent pinks, delicately veined greens and brooding blood-reds. Once this happy field was awake and watered and bathed in sunlight, Imogene would go to school.

Each day after school, Imogene took a wagon of orchids across the bay on the Staten Island Ferry and delivered them to fancy flower shops in Manhattan.

The ferry captain's name was Edd Neck, or Big Edd. Big Edd steered the boat with one hand and told funny stories over the intercom. Badly drawn tattoos covered his arms, a moon-sized bald spot capped his head, and he kind of smelled like old cheese. Ladies sometimes coughed or wrinkled their noses when he walked by.

Imogene, on the other hand, adored him. In fact, he was her best friend. If you think it's odd for a young girl to be best friends with a stinky boat captain, consider the facts: Imogene was an eleven-year-old girl living with her white-haired grandfather in an orchid greenhouse. While Imogene's curious life intrigued her classmates, it made her shy too, and needless to say, she did not have a lot of friends her own age. As everyone knows, shyness and loneliness often come hand in hand, and companionship sometimes comes in unlikely forms.

One frigid Friday afternoon last December, when Imogene came on board with her orchid-filled wagon, Big Edd let one of his crewmen steer the boat and came over to admire the flowers.

"Those are nice," he told her. "I wish I had a lady friend; I'd buy her that bright yellow one."

"Why don't you buy it for yourself?" Imogene asked. "For the steering room or something." She couldn't actually imagine Big Edd having a living room, or a house, for that matter. He seemed to live on the ferry.

"It's not the same thing, Blossom," sighed Big Edd. "Blossom" was Big Edd's nickname for Imogene.

"I guess not," said Imogene, feeling sad for Big Edd, who

looked very woebegone at the moment. "Maybe someday you'll get a girlfriend."

"Ha, not me," said Big Edd. "No woman in her right mind would want me for a husband. No one's ever looked twice. And anyway, my standards are too high. A dame has to be pretty gorgeous to catch my eye. So the river and the sea are my ladies, and they always will be."

Imogene got off the ferry in Manhattan and made her deliveries, her wagon bump-bump-bumping along the uneven sidewalks. It was cold and dark on the ride home, and she pulled her coat tightly around her as the nearly empty boat lurched away from the dock.

Halfway across the bay, the door to Big Edd's steering room swung open and he stomped out.

"Larry—what is that?" he asked.

"What's what, boss?" said Larry, who was one of Big Edd's crewmen. He sat on a bench outside the cabin, eating a hoagie.

"That God-awful yowling noise," said Big Edd. "Like a cat got caught in the engine or something."

Larry stopped chewing. "Yeah," he said after a moment. "I hear it. But it's coming from out there, not the engine room."

The men marched out onto the deck and peered into the night. Imogene ran after them.

"Oh, man," said Big Edd, wincing. "If I didn't know any

better, I'd say that was a dame with the world's worst voice, trying to sing an opera."

Imogene's heart gave a leap. "It is a woman," she said. "Look over there. She's sitting on those rocks in the middle of the bay."

"You got X-ray night vision or something?" said Big Edd. "Where?"

"Right there," cried Imogene, pointing, and indeed there sat a woman on some rocks in the distance, waving at the boat. "She's the one making that noise. It looks like she needs rescuing." Imogene looked again and blushed and said, "Oh."

"Whaddya mean, 'oh'?" said Big Edd.

"Um, I think she's naked," said Imogene.

"All right," yelled Larry. "Let's go help her out!"

"Just a minute," said Big Edd, squinting. "All I see is some sort of lumpy shape. Could be an animal or a big hunk of trash. Get back into the cabin, Larry, and call animal control or the coast guard or something. We're staying right on course; we'll all get fired if we don't stick to the schedule." Larry looked very disappointed but followed Big Edd's order.

"It's not an animal—it's a woman!" cried Imogene. "I swear."

Big Edd looked at her queerly. "You feeling okay, Blossom? I'm worried about you. Maybe you oughta get your eyes checked out by the school nurse."

He followed Larry back into the steering room. The Staten Island Ferry chugged along into the night.

Imogene stared out over the railing at the woman on the rocks. She had stopped singing and was watching the ferry intently. Suddenly she dove into the black water and there was a flash of a fat silver fish tail—and then she disappeared.

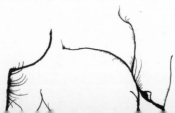

It seemed like a dream to Imogene the next morning. She woke up thinking about the glint of the woman's skin in the pale moonlight. After breakfast, Imogene sat on a bag of soil in the greenhouse and thought some more about the woman and restlessly tore up dead orchid leaves. Her hands didn't want to stop moving. Shred, shred, toss. Shred, shred, toss.

Blue pipe smoke curled up into the air from behind Grandfather's Saturday-morning newspaper.

"Go for a walk," he told Imogene.

"But it's cold out," Imogene protested.

"Yes, it is," said Grandfather. "But you're driving me bananas. Go outside until your hands are too numb to shred those leaves, and then you may come inside."

Imogene scowled as she wound her scarf around her neck. She knew that Grandfather was only joking, but why did he have to be so weird all the time? Soon she was kicking seashells and rocks down on the beach. In the distance the ferry was making one of its early-morning trips to Manhattan; it glided over the water and vanished into the fog.

That's when she heard it.

The yowl; that awful, hilarious, cat-in-a-ferry-engine yowl from the previous night. Except this time there was the yowl, followed by some piteous sobs, and then the yowl again. Then more sobs. The noises came from under the dock; Imogene ran out onto it and peered underneath.

There sat the naked woman from the night before, waist-deep in water, crying and singing to herself.

"I *knew* you were real," Imogene said, forgetting to say hello or introduce herself. "I tried to get them to rescue you last night. Aren't you freezing?"

The woman looked up at her with woeful yellow eyes. "I'm always cold," she said, and slapped at the water.

"So why don't you come out of the water, then?" Imogene frowned.

The woman slapped at the water again—a bit childishly, Imogene thought.

"I can't—I mean, I don't want to," the woman said.

Imogene suddenly remembered the fish tail flashing in the moonlight the night before and things began to make more sense. She took a deep breath.

"Are you a mermaid?"

"Of course I am," snapped the mermaid. "Why else would I be sitting in icy water on a day like this?" Her face rumpled up and there were tears again. "All I wanted was for him to notice me."

"Who?" asked Imogene.

"The captain of that vessel," whimpered the woman.

"You mean Big Edd?" Imogene was baffled. And after a

perplexed minute, she asked: "Were you trying to sing to him?"

"Ye-e-e-e-s," hiccuped the woman. "But it's useless. Look at me! I can't sing a note, all the algae has made my golden hair slimy and green, and I have a face that would stop a clock. People always mistake me for some sort of homely beast. One time a sailor threw up over the side of a boat when he saw me up close."

Imogene looked more closely. Indeed, the mermaid was quite ugly.

"But why do you want Big Edd to notice you so badly?" Imogene asked, still stumped. Big Edd himself had said that no woman in her right mind had ever looked twice at him.

"I just *need* him to," said the mermaid mysteriously, and sobs shook her wretched blue body again.

Imogene sat upright on the dock and thought for a moment. It was turning out to be a very unusual morning. This mermaid appeared to be in love with Big Edd of all people.

If this was "love," Imogene reasoned further, it certainly was a peculiar state of affairs. She wondered why everyone made such a big deal about love if it made people wail and yowl and sit waist-deep in ice-cold dirty bay water.

What Imogene did not know: this was not just any old mermaid; she was a Lorelei. Clearly a defective one—but a Lorelei all the same.

What Imogene did know: Big Edd was her best friend and he was lonely. And lo and behold, this woman seemed terribly interested in him. Wasn't a homely mermaid better than nothing? Imogene peered down over the side of the dock again.

"I'm going to help you," she said to the mermaid.

"How?"

"I'm going to get Big Edd to fall in love with you," Imogene said. She didn't know quite how she was going to accomplish this, but there had to be a way.

"Really?" The woman swept a gummy green tendril of hair from her eyes and gave Imogene an ingratiating smile, her teeth a decaying keyboard with some of the keys missing. This would clearly not be an easy challenge. "How?"

"I'm going to think up a plan," Imogene told her. "Meet me here tomorrow at the same time."

"Wonderful," said the mermaid. "I'll start practicing a new song."

"Let's try something different," Imogene said tactfully. "I'll come up with something good."

She ran home to begin her research.

That night after dinner, Grandfather's pipe smoke rose again from behind his favorite evening reading: a beleaguered old movie magazine from 1953. Imogene stood tentatively in front of him.

"Grandfather," she said.

"Yes?"

"What makes a woman pretty?"

"Hmmm?"

"What makes a man notice a woman?"

Grandfather put down his magazine and looked wistfully into space. "A fine set of chops, I'd say."

Imogene paused, not quite knowing what to do with this information. "What else?" she asked.

There was a long silence, and then: "A fine set of gams, I'd say."

"Chops" and "gams"—what was he talking about? Imogene gave up. She poked impatiently at Grandfather's magazine. "Why do you read this same old fifty-year-old magazine all the time?" she demanded.

"Someone put a lot of work into making it all those years ago," Grandfather said contentedly. "The least I can do is give it some attention. And look at Marilyn Monroe there on the front cover. How could a man ever weary of her?"

And he put the magazine up in front of his face again.

Imogene stared at the woman on the cover. Marilyn Monroe, movie star, had bouncy blond curls. The picture gave Imogene an idea.

She counted her saved allowance money and then went to sleep.

Mondays usually come too quickly; in this case, it meandered and dawdled and took its sweet time in arriving. After school on Monday afternoon, Imogene ran with her wagon to the ferry, clumsily bouncing some of the orchids out onto the ground and leaving a trail of petals, moss, and leaves in her wake. As the ferry pulled away from the dock, she tied the wagon to some chairs and looked for Big Edd.

He was in his steerage cabin, laughing with some of his crewmen. The cabin windows were steamed up with breath and body heat. Imogene wondered how they could see the river at all and grew anxious as the boat made its way into the middle of the bay. If Big Edd stayed in that bog of a room, he would miss the surprise she had cooked up for him.

She knocked on one of the windows.

"Hey, Blossom," said Big Edd, opening his door. "How's my best girl?"

"Can you come out for a minute?" Imogene said. "I want to show you something."

"Like what, another naked lady on the rocks?" asked Larry. "The coast guard was real excited to get out to those rocks the other night and find nothing there."

"Aw, shut your trap, Larry," said Big Edd. "She's just a kid."

"Just come with me," Imogene begged Big Edd, pulling on his sleeve. The boat was getting close to the mermaid's rocks.

"Uh-uh," said Big Edd. "It's freezing out there. I'm staying in here where it's nice and cozy. You should come in too, Blossom, unless you wanna turn into a Popsicle."

The rocks came into view, and once again, the Lorelei lounged on top of them.

"Oh!" cried Imogene, running out onto the deck. "You're going to miss it! Hurry up!"

"Forget it," said Big Edd. "Knock on the door once you're done running 'round in the cold," and he closed the steamy door just as they passed the rocks.

The mermaid's head had been stuffed into a perky wig of corkscrew blond curls, removed from a thrift-store dummy and purchased by Imogene the day before. Imogene saw with dismay that the woman had put the wig on *backward*, for heaven's sake. It really was quite a dreadful effect.

By the time the boat went back in the other direction, the mermaid—and the wig—was long gone.

⚉ ⚉ ⚉

"I *knew* it wouldn't work," wailed the mermaid the next day. She took off the drenched, sorry wig and threw it into the oily water under the dock.

"That's because you had it on the wrong way," Imogene told her. "If you'd worn it right, you would have looked like Marilyn Monroe."

"Who is Marilyn Monroe?" sniffed the mermaid.

"An olden-days movie star," Imogene said. "My grandfather's been looking at a picture of her practically every day for fifty years, so she must have been doing something right.

If we make you look like her, I bet that Big Edd will fall in love with you. So put it back on, and try this." She handed the woman a tube.

"What is it?" said the mermaid, sniffing the tube.

"Lipstick," Imogene told her impatiently.

The mermaid opened it and gave it a little lick. "What do you do with it?"

"You put it on your lips," explained Imogene. "It's red, just like Marilyn Monroe used to wear. Now sit out there on the rocks this afternoon, and I'll make sure that Big Edd sees you."

The plan was, of course, an abject failure.

When the ferry glided past the mermaid's rocks again, the wig was on *sideways* this time; the lipstick was a disaster beyond explaining; once again, Big Edd refused to leave that steam bath of a steering room.

The final insult: a passenger threw a beer can in the Lorelei's direction, beaning her right between the eyes.

Imogene was at her wit's end. This project was turning out to be an awful lot of work. But Big Edd is worth it, she reminded herself, thinking about how forlorn he'd looked when talking about wanting a "lady friend."

Having no one else to ask for advice, she returned to Grandfather.

There he sat in the shack next to the greenhouse, drinking coffee and still reading the morning newspaper. A record spun lazily on an old windup phonograph on the dirt floor, making comforting pops and murmurs.

"Grandfather," Imogene said, sitting down in her usual spot on top of a soil sack.

"Yes, child," he said absentmindedly.

"What do you think is the prettiest thing about Marilyn Monroe?"

"Hmmm?"

"Is it her puffy hair?" Imogene pressed. "Or her red lips? How did she get men to look at her?"

Grandfather put down his paper and thought for a moment. "No, it wasn't about those things, although they were nice," he said, a little smile on his lips. "It was her voice."

"Her *voice*?"

"Yes," said Grandfather. "Listen to this," he added, getting up and shuffling across the room. He pulled an old record off a shelf and placed it on the phonograph player. "This is one of Miss Monroe's most famous songs, called 'The River of No Return.'"

Imogene listened for a while.

"She just sounds out of breath to me," she said crossly. "I don't see what's so great about her."

"A million chaps would disagree with you there," said Grandfather, listening happily. "That voice could lure you across the globe and back."

This statement intrigued Imogene. She looked down at the phonograph player.

"Can I borrow that tomorrow after school?" she asked.

చిప్ చిప్ చిప్

The phonograph player was heavier than it looked, and the logistics, of course, were nearly impossible. Getting it wet would be a disaster. Imogene wheeled it out onto the dock in her wagon with her orchids.

"Listen," she told the mermaid, who sat shivering under the dock, and she wound up the player and played the breathy lullaby.

> There is a river called the River of No Return
> Sometimes it's peaceful and sometimes wild
> and free
> Love is a trav'ler on the River of No Return
> Swept on forever to be lost in the stormy sea.

The mermaid listened intently; she was still and quiet. She looked almost pretty in her quietness, the way that old broken china dolls are pretty. When the song was over, she wanted to hear it again, and when it was over for the second time, she asked:

"What is it?"

"It's your new voice," Imogene told her solemnly.

The phonograph player was suddenly light; the mermaid balanced it on her head easily as she swam toward her rocky perch in the bay, skimming the water's surface like a petal in the current.

As the mermaid disappeared into the silver winter fog, Imogene felt a pang of melancholy. Would Big Edd forget all about her when he fell in love with the mermaid? Would she lose her best friend? She knew that you weren't supposed to be selfish about sharing your friends; you were supposed to want what was best for them, which is why she wanted to help him find a "lady friend" in the first place. But the idea of losing him still bothered her.

She dragged the wagon to the ferry docks. And then she did something she'd never done before: instead of getting on the boat to do her job, Imogene stood on the dock and watched Big Edd's ferry lurch out into the water toward Manhattan. Then she turned and went home.

Even though it was only four in the afternoon, she crawled into bed and didn't get up for dinner.

❀ ❀ ❀

She woke with a start and it was still black-dark outside. Grandfather was standing over her, smoking his pipe.

"What's wrong?" Imogene said, raising herself up on her elbows.

"How did you know, child?" asked Grandfather.

"How did I know what?"

"To stay off the ferry yesterday."

Imogene lay back down. "I didn't feel good, that's all," she mumbled. "I'll deliver the flowers this afternoon."

"Well, have a look at this," said Grandfather, and he shook out an early edition of the morning newspaper above her.

Imogene took it and squinted at the headline.

The Staten Island Sentinel

STATEN ISLAND FERRY CRASHES IN BAY

"FERRY CAPTAIN A BELOVED MEMBER OF STATEN ISLAND COMMUNITY, SAYS NEIGHBOR"

Edward 'Big Edd' Neck, captain of the Staten Island Ferry who is missing and feared dead in yesterday's mysterious wreck, is a beloved member of the Staten Island neighborhood where he has lived since he was born, says his next-door neighbor, Mrs. Myrtle McButton.

"Such a dear young man," said Mrs. McButton, 83. "He always came over for my Sunday night meat loaf dinners. I always told him, 'Edward, you need to find a wife. Don't be so picky.' I hope he finds a nice wife in heaven, who knows how to make a good meat loaf."

BOAT FLOODED, CAPTAIN MISSING, FEARED DROWNED

CURIOUS ARRAY OF CLUES FOUND AT SITE OF WRECKAGE

A tattered blond wig and a bewildering array of shining silver fish scales are among the wreckage clues that investigators will be examining as they determine the cause of the Staten Island Ferry's crash, said a source familiar with the proceedings.

"Who knows if these items are related to the accident," said Police Commissioner Larry Plotzky at a press conference last night. "All sorts of god-forsaken things wash up around here. Just the other day, a big crate of xylophones washed up on the beach—who ever heard of something like that? But we gotta look at every clue, no matter how weird."

The feeling drained from Imogene's hands, and before Grandfather could stop her, Imogene was running outside, the cold air burning her throat. She ran until she reached the rocky beach and then the dock.

The mermaid wasn't there.

What *was* there instead: Grandfather's phonograph player, closed and safe and snug in the sand, covered in white seashells—a thank-you gift from the deadly Staten Island Lorelei.

Never, *ever* help a mermaid, even if you have your own reasons for doing so and even if you come across one as seemingly helpless and hopeless as the one in this story. No good will come of it, *especially* if the mermaid indeed turns out to be a deadly Lorelei—and most humans, no matter how knowledgeable, cannot tell the difference. You know, as Imogene did not, that the Lorelei have only one purpose: to sink ships and claim their passengers.

Another fact about the Lorelei: they often attempt to bewitch a boat's captain. It's like capturing the king in chess. Once you have the heart of the captain, the boat's more likely to go down, and everyone on board becomes your prize.

Imogene's Lorelei may have been nasty to look at and wretched and a bad singer, but she was no dummy. Enchantment takes many guises, and she knew that she could control people by making them feel sorry for her. As you saw, it was just as easy to trick and manipulate humans with ugliness as it would have been to use beauty.

Imogene never saw Big Edd again, and neither did anyone else. But she and Grandfather did honor his memory in their own way. Someday, if you just happen to walk past a flower shop, stop inside and ask the owner if they carry a rare, Staten Island–grown, bright yellow variety of orchid known as Big Edd's Ballad.

A Short Note on Perfume

Women have long relied on perfumes to make themselves appealing. Long ago, the Lorelei used a special kind of perfume to help lure sailors to their deaths; it smelled like the freshest sea air and made men think wistfully of their youth.

Clearly the Staten Island Lorelei in Imogene's tale hadn't known about this scent, or she wouldn't have had such a hard time luring Big Edd to his end.

A note to young ladies (and pass this on to your mothers also): fairies are fond of flower-like scents or those evoking wood. Therefore, wearing certain perfumes might help you garner favor with local fairies.

These days, the following eaux de toilette are pretty easy to find in your pharmacy:

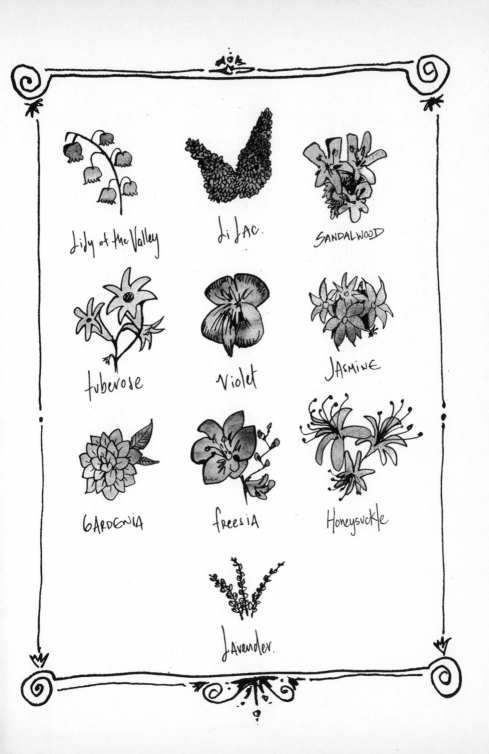

If the perfumes are too expensive, you can always try a bit of rosewater or orange blossom water—or even fresh lemon juice. One dab behind each ear and one on the inside of each wrist should do the trick.

Fairies also like the smell of smoldering embers and may visit your fireplace long after the fire has been put out and you've gone to bed. Any perfumes that have smoky traces in them are equally adored.

The Blight of Pools

Not all bodies of water make good habitats for fairies. You might think that pools are among the best inventions of all time, especially during summer, but they are absolutely poisonous to most winged fairies. The chlorine in the water, which turns your hair green if you spend too much time in the pool, does far worse things to fairies: when they are splashed with chlorine water, it melts their wings, like acid.

Also, fairies often confuse pools with ponds and use them for drinking water, which painfully dissolves them from the inside.

If your family has a pool in the backyard, make sure that it's covered up when not in use; you may save a fairy's life.

Trolls, on the other hand, have a far stronger constitution than their distant winged cousins; they love your pool. In fact, if you leave it uncovered at night, they may come and bathe in it, leaving a fine, foul mess for you to deal with in the morning.

Why Human Hair Turns Gray

Although they likely didn't know it, Imogene and her grandfather were dealing with not one but two types of fairies in Tale No. 6. The first, of course, was the Lorelei—but the second type is known as the Fading fairy.

As you know, when humans age, their hair turns gray or silver or even white. This actually has nothing to do with natural causes; the Fading fairies are draining and stealing the rich colors for themselves.

The Fades are the most widespread of all winged fairy breeds, literally dwelling on every continent—wherever there is a human population—and yet very few people have ever heard of them. They are so tiny that it is difficult for even people with the sharpest fairy sight to spot them.

This is how they got their name: the Fades are vibrantly colored when they are born, but as they age, they fade to black-and-white, like an old newspaper—and then to nothing. One of the few fairy breeds that seem unable to manipulate time in some way, the Fades desperately usurp human hues to keep from disappearing entirely. They drain one hair at a time while a person sleeps and store the color in bottles, from which they sip as necessary.

Clearly the Fades had been visiting Imogene's grandfather for years, since his hair was entirely white at the time of the story.

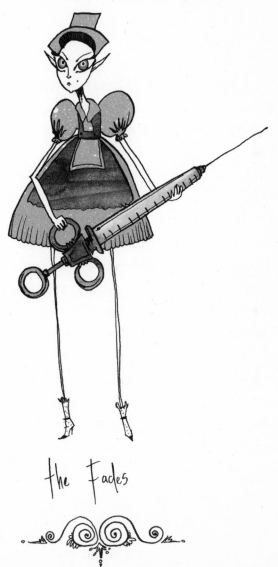

the Fades

Why Fairies Covet
Human Babies

And now we travel from old age to extreme youth.

As you learned in "Time in the Fairy World," many fairies love being young, but weirdly, they often dislike their own babies. Many fairy babies are hideous-looking, even ones that will eventually grow into beautiful winged creatures someday.

So, in many cases, a fairy swaps her own ugly baby for a pretty human baby. The fairy baby left in human hands is known as a changeling. Of course, the human mother doesn't know that the baby is a changeling; she thinks that it's her own child. That's because the fairies have cast a spell over the ugly fairy baby to make it look human.

Changeling swaps happen frequently, and when the babies have grown, the fairies reclaim them, leaving the human mothers with nothing. No one knows what happens to the human babies who are taken in the first place—although in the old days, many children would abruptly turn up at country orphanages, speaking strange languages that no one had heard before. Perhaps the fairies keep the human babies until they reclaim their own and then turn the human children out into the world to fend for themselves.

If there is evidence of fairy activity near your home and you're worried they might steal your baby brother or sister, link a daisy chain along the edge of his or her crib, just in case.

But sometimes there is nothing you can do to prevent a fairy kidnapping, as you'll see in Tale No. 7.

Tale No. 7
Ball Lightning at Coney Island

The day that Lucius was born, the hospital burned down. Well, not the whole hospital—just one wing of the building, actually—but it was still upsetting for a lot of people, and this is how it happened:

It was a quiet, heavy-aired summer night, the sort where fanning yourself with a sheet of paper does no good and the mosquitoes seem fatter and meaner than ever. Even the heat lightning that flickered in the sky seemed cranky and listless; then, suddenly, what appeared to be a ball of lightning shot out of the swollen purple sky and smacked into the side of the hospital, setting it on fire.

This was according to one of the baby ward's night nurses, who just happened to be holding Lucius and singing him a little lullaby and looking out the window when the lightning ball came. Miraculously, no one was hurt, but no one really believed the night nurse's story.

"There's no such thing as ball lightning," said a whole host of scientists and meteorologists and firemen who'd been called in to inspect the scene; they even made her take a lie detector test—*which* she passed, I might add. But they still called the nurse a liar ("Was she *drunk?*") and took away her job; the official cause of the fire was eventually attributed to faulty wiring in the hospital's basement.

Lightning seemed to follow Lucius wherever he went. First his nursery school had an incident; then, when he was three, the roof of the next-door neighbor's house, where Lucius was playing with a friend, caught fire one stormy afternoon. When Lucius's backyard tree house went up in flames a year later, his older sister, Cecilia, began to worry about her brother's welfare.

No one ever suspected Lucius of any foul play; after all, he was the sweetest child anyone had ever seen, a quiet boy with downy black hair and still hands and almost-silver eyes. Mirror-colored eyes, in fact. Like a magpie, Lucius liked objects with a sharp shine to them: tinfoil in the sunshine, a knife gleaming in the glow of a table candle.

But he *did* have his oddnesses, to be fair. For one thing, he didn't really start speaking until he was two years old, and then the words didn't *quite* sound like English. In fact, they sounded like no language that anyone had ever heard before, but soon he learned to say "Mama" and "Papa" and "dog" too, and everyone breathed a sigh of relief.

One afternoon, Cecilia was babysitting Lucius, who was six by then; they were playing in the garden of their family's West Village town house. It was raining but they didn't care; the floors inside had just been waxed and the house stunk.

"Get off the picnic table," yelled Cecilia, who

was eleven. Lucius teetered on one end of it, threatening to pitch it forward like a seesaw.

"Nothing can hurt me," yelled Lucius, waving a plastic sword. "I'm invincible!"

A flash of lightning lit the sky, followed by a terrific crack of thunder, and suddenly Cecilia saw a ball of fire surging from the sky toward the yard.

"Lucius!" she screamed, and tackled him off the end of the table. They fell to the ground, her body covering his, and the fireball flew over them and hit the ground, leaving a black, smoldering hole in the grass. Lucius began to cry, and later that evening their parents were hysterical.

"My babies!" wailed their mother, holding Lucius in her arms. "What would I have done if that bolt of lightning had taken you both away from me?"

"It was a ball of lightning, not a bolt," Cecilia told her.

"Lightning doesn't come in balls," sniffed her mother. "But what does it matter? You're both safe, thank God."

It was a happy ending until it wasn't: the next morning when the family woke up, Lucius was missing.

"Most kids turn up within twenty-four hours," the detective told Cecilia's parents down at the police station. They'd been there all day. Cecilia sat on a bench outside his office while the adults talked. One of the policemen had a TV on his desk, and the local news blared at top volume.

Cecilia's mother came out of the detective's office.

"Mom, look," said Cecilia. "There was a fire at Vesuvio Bakery."

Vesuvio was the family's favorite bakery in SoHo, a neighborhood east of theirs. Bright mint-green paint covered the store's wooden facade and inside it was dark and calm, the sort of place where you told secrets.

"Lucius loves that place," Cecilia's mother said. "Those pecan honey buns. So sticky. What a mess," and then she started crying again.

On the way home, Cecilia couldn't stop thinking about the fire at Vesuvio. The idea of it nagged at her. She brought it up again.

"Restaurant kitchens catch fire all the time," snapped her father. "Now stop talking about it. There are more important things to think about."

Cecilia frowned, but she kept quiet. When the family got home, she went upstairs into her room, and when the house was dark and filled with anxious sleep, she silently stuffed a sweatshirt and a jar with her allowance savings ($42.67) into her school backpack. She dozed on her bed until a pale light began to seep into the sky in the east.

Down in the dawn-lit kitchen, she taped a note to the refrigerator.

Then Cecilia silently slipped out the front door.

It was as she suspected.

A round burn mark—about three feet wide—blackened

the side of the Vesuvio Bakery. Cecilia went inside, where the baker and his wife were cleaning up after the fire.

"Excuse me—have you seen this boy?" she asked them, holding up a picture of Lucius that had been taken on Cape Cod the summer before.

The baker shook his head. "All we've seen today is firemen, young lady," he said. "We're closed, so scram."

"Were there pecan honey buns on the premises before the fire?" Cecilia pressed.

"What a funny question," said the baker, sweeping some ashes into a dustbin. "There are always pecan honey buns on the premises. Although we noticed that a bunch of them were missing from the tray last night, before the fire."

Lucius had definitely been there.

Cecilia went to a deli next door, bought a root beer and some peanut butter crackers, and sat at the counter, waiting for her next clue. She drank and ate, watching the television above the deli meat section and trying to look casual. She bought another root beer and tried to make it last.

At about two o'clock, another clue came in over a newscast on the deli television.

"A mysterious fire has just closed down the Delancey Street–Essex Street subway station," said a very concerned reporter who was wearing too much brown lipstick. "Police suspect arson and are investigating at this very moment."

Cecilia ran outside and hailed a taxi. She was only eleven, but everyone knows how to hail a taxi in New York City. I know dogs who can hail taxis in this town, for goodness' sake. Ten minutes later she stood in front of the Delancey Street–Essex Street subway station. Yellow police tape zigzagged across the entrance and a group of firemen were just pulling away on their enormous red truck. A circular burn mark blackened the subway stairs.

Cecilia sat down with a thump on the curb and eavesdropped as the police talked to neighbors and witnesses.

"It was like when you pour gasoline on a grill," said one man, who owned a kebab stand across the street. "Whoosh! A big ball of fire out of nowhere. And then it was gone."

The sugar from the root beer was starting to give Cecilia a headache. She looked up at the wall next to the subway entrance.

A slightly charred advertisement for Coney Island hung to the left of the stairs.

I've heard it said before that all we really have in this world is our instincts. After all, human instincts are strong, and in ancient times, we had to rely on them for our very survival. These days we often underappreciate them and certainly don't use them enough.

At that moment, as Cecilia stared up at the poster,

her instincts were telling her that her six-year-old brother was on that subway, en route to the rickety old Cyclone, where fun times were apparently back. And while she didn't know *why* Lucius was going there or why these balls of lightning were following him every hour—or why they were plaguing him at *all*, for that matter—she knew that she needed to help him.

When the policemen snipped away the yellow tape from the subway entrance, she went down the stairs and got on the train to Coney Island.

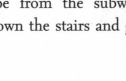

No black smoke hung in the air above Coney Island when Cecilia emerged from the subway, which was a good thing for everyone in the area besides her. Until she heard about or saw evidence of the next Lucius fire, she had no way to find him.

I don't know if you've ever been to Coney Island, but it is not really an island at all; rather, it's a beachside town in Brooklyn, that is home to a very old and famous amusement park. There is a blaze of video arcades and all sorts of creaky rides and places where you can buy thick bales of gritty cotton candy.

Under different circumstances, these diversions might have been tempting for an eleven-year-old girl, but today Cecilia was too tired and worried to pay attention. She needed a rest, and after walking around for a little while looking for a small, black-haired, silver-eyed boy, she ducked inside a public library.

"Can I help you find anything?" asked a librarian, shaking Cecilia's shoulder gently.

"No, thank you," said Cecilia blearily. She had fallen asleep in a plastic chair, curled up like a cat. A fluorescent light buzzed idly overhead.

"The library is for reading, not sleeping," the librarian told her. "Let's find you a nice book."

Cecilia thought for a minute.

"Actually, do you have any books on lightning that comes in balls?" she said. "Oh, and maybe a book about Coney Island."

This is what an encyclopedia had to say under the entry "Ball Lightning":

Given inconsistencies and the lack of reliable data, the true nature of ball lightning is still unknown. Historically, ball lightning was often regarded as a fantasy or a hoax. Reports of the phenomenon were dismissed for lack of physical evidence and were often regarded the same way as UFO sightings. Natural ball lightning appears infrequently and unpredictably and is therefore rarely (if ever truly) photographed.

And yet, according to the encyclopedia, many people had reported sightings: in India, in Africa—even Czar Nicholas II of Russia had reported seeing ball lightning as a child. If there had been so many sightings, Cecilia wondered, why did no one believe that it existed? People never wanted to believe in anything. She put down the encyclopedia and picked up the book about Coney Island.

Here was an especially interesting and relevant passage:

Coney Island is most closely associated with the image of its

iconic roller coaster, the Cyclone.
The Cyclone holds the unique honor
of having been hit by lightning more
times than any other roller coaster
in the world: 46 times since the ride
opened in 1927.

Cecilia's heart pounded. She looked out the window. Clouds swelled in the sky again, turning it purple and gray and green, like an ugly bruise. She grabbed her backpack and hurried out of the library. On the front steps, she almost ran smack into the library's custodian, who dropped a bucket of dirty mop water down the stairs.

"You'll break your neck, running around like that," he hollered. "Where's the fire?"

"At the Cyclone," Cecilia shouted back, and she ran and she didn't stop running until she reached the amusement park where the Cyclone lived.

∽ ⸎ ∽ ⸎ ∽

It looked like the skeleton of a huge, sleeping animal, a dragon, maybe, or something worse.

The fence around the Cyclone was like a cage, keeping the animal inside. The park was closed and empty, and Cecilia

had to walk quite a way before she found a hole in the fence big enough to crawl through.

The sky was almost midnight-black and she heard a rumble. At first she thought that rumble was thunder, but it didn't sound like any thunder she'd ever heard before. It sounded like a deep, ominous death rattle from the belly of the earth. Then Cecilia looked up and realized that the rumble had not come from the sky or the earth.

It was the sound of the Cyclone coming to life.

A set of coaster cars began to inch up the arch of the Cyclone's spine, like a yellow and red caterpillar. The metal wheels groaned and creaked. Suddenly a soft shape in the first car caught Cecilia's attention.

"Lucius!" she screamed.

The boy turned his head and looked down at his sister. He waved gaily.

"Come down from there right now," shouted Cecilia before she realized how ridiculous that sounded. A flash of white light filled the sky, and by the time the thunder had cracked, Cecilia climbed into the next set of Cyclone cars, which shuddered as they lurched up the ramp.

Lucius's car reached the peak, hovered at the top for a moment, and then plunged down the track. Cecilia heard him scream with glee and soon her car had reached the peak. Her stomach knotted up when she saw the drop, and a second later the car hurtled downward. The smell of painted metal and ozone filled her nostrils as the roller coaster jolted her left and right and the park flashed by.

Soon the car slowed and turned upward again and began to climb the next steep hill. Cecilia wiped her eyes and saw Lucius's car ahead of her on the ramp.

"CeCe! CeCe!" he shouted down to her. "Isn't this fun?"

Just then a blinding flash of lightning and a crack of thunder happened at the exact same moment, and out

of the sky came three or four fiery balls. But instead of shooting like bullets across the sky, they hovered—dawdled, even—like dandelion fluff blowing in the breeze toward the Cyclone.

Lucius stood up in his car.

"CeCe—aren't they pretty?" he yelled. The lightning balls bathed him in yellow light.

"Sit down; are you crazy?" cried Cecilia, and then his car reached the top and the fiery balls floated in and surrounded him. The light burned so bright that Cecilia had to cover her eyes, and then there was another clap of thunder and Lucius's car raced down the ramp on the other side.

This time it was empty.

Eventually the police came, and fire trucks and ambulances too. They looked everywhere to see if Lucius had fallen out of the car (he had not) or been burned up by the lightning (which, again, he had not; in fact, the roller coaster car in which he'd ridden had absolutely no evidence of a lightning strike at all). In the end, they concluded that Cecilia had been lying (sound familiar?)—not just about seeing Lucius on the roller coaster, but also about the lightning balls.

Because Cecilia had been right back in the Coney Island

public library: people never want to believe in anything that they can't explain.

ᐧᐧᐧ ᐧᐧᐧ ᐧᐧᐧ

I know that this story is a little different from the other tales in this book. But I'm willing to bet that you knew fairies were somehow involved with those lightning balls that followed poor Lucius from the day of his birth to the day he vanished.

When it comes to explaining ball lightning, scientists are both wrong and right.

As you know, they are wrong when they claim these fiery spheres are hoaxes or fictions.

But this is where scientists are right: ball lightning is not lightning at all.

Ball lightning is a fierce field of electricity that surrounds a breed of fairy known as the Pyrofairies. The prefix "pyro" comes from the Greek word for "fire."

Very little is known about the Pyrofairies, which are possibly the most elusive creatures in the fairy world. As you saw from the encyclopedia entry in the Coney Island library, there have been Pyrofairy sightings across the globe, and fairy experts in every culture have different theories about the breed's origin. In Mexico, for example, fairyologists believe that Pyrofairies are direct descendants of an early Aztec sun god named Tezcatlipoca; in Egypt, they're believed to have sprung from the early Egyptian sun god Ra. No one knows for sure.

What all Pyrofairies in every country have in common: every once in a while, they become attracted to a child, and eventually that child disappears. I have researched nearly every recorded Pyrofairy case, and these are the facts:

Over the years, each targeted, or "marked," child followed by Pyrofairies looked vaguely like Lucius, with dark hair and mirror-colored eyes.

Each spoke in a strange language before learning the language of his or her parents.

All "marked" children disappeared when they were six or so, usually amidst a storm during which "ball lightning" was reported.

For the most part, these children are very attracted to fires and often get into trouble for playing with matches when they are little. Also, they never get sunburned at the beach, even if their skin is as pale as milk.

There is only one conclusion to be drawn: these children are not human children at all; they are changelings—which, as you learned earlier in this book, are fairy babies that have been secretly left in the place of human ones. The Pyrofairies track down their offspring about six years after swapping them out—usually by luring them away from their foster homes to a

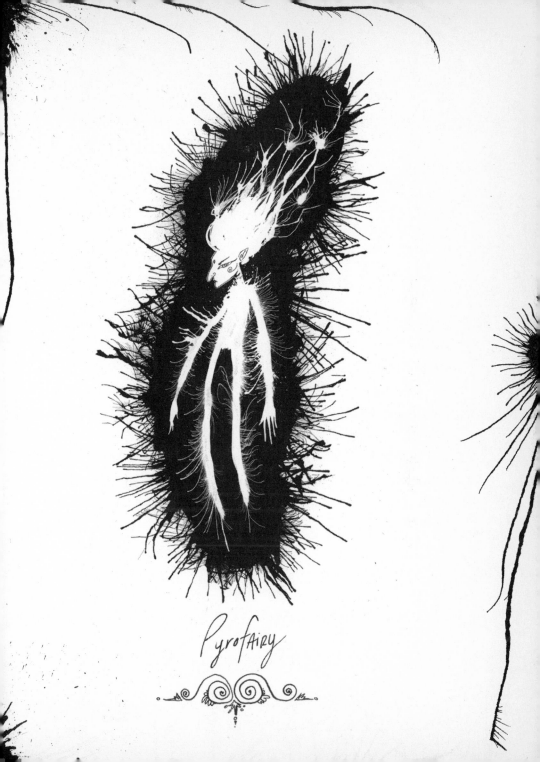

PyroFairy

high peak and seizing them. This is what happened to Lucius at the top of the Cyclone.

In the meantime, the fire fairies check in on the changelings every year or so, leaving a scalding calling card each time.

Lucius's disappearance is still listed as "unsolved" in police files.

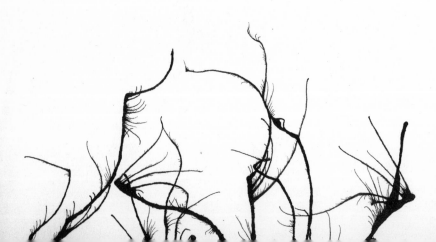

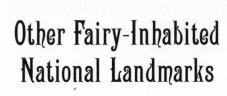

Other Fairy-Inhabited National Landmarks

Coney Island is considered by many to be a national landmark; in fact, some historical parts of the amusement park and its old signs are now part of the Smithsonian's National Air and Space Museum in Washington, D.C.

As you probably suspected, Coney Island is not the only national landmark where considerable fairy activity has taken place. Below are a few other such places.

Mount Rushmore

Sixty-foot sculptures of the faces of Presidents George Washington, Thomas Jefferson, Theodore Roosevelt, and Abraham Lincoln are carved into the granite side of this peak, representing the first 150 years of the United States' history. It took sculptor

Gutzon Borglum and four hundred workers fourteen long years to make these carvings.

Well, it would have taken *twice* as long if the Black Hills dwarves hadn't stepped in to help—for a price, of course. Borglum cut a deal with this local dwarf tribe to continue the hard work at night, when no photographers were around. Skilled granite carvers, these dwarves eventually introduced Borglum's workers to all sorts of unusual carving techniques. Of course, no records detail how much Borglum paid the dwarves, but a trusted associate later told his wife from his deathbed that Borglum paid them about half a million dollars.

People often say it's a miracle that not a single worker died during the construction of Mount Rushmore; after all, two million tons of rock were dynamited off the peak—rather dangerous work. Actually, this "miracle" is also the work of the Black Hills dwarves, who cast a protective spell over the workers as part of their deal with Borglum.

Unfortunately for him, Borglum gypped the dwarves out of their final payment and they angrily reversed the protective spell. Not surprisingly, Borglum died shortly thereafter and his son had to complete the project for him.

The Chrysler Building

If you point a pair of binoculars at the top of this beautiful Art Deco skyscraper in New York City, you will see several menacing steel American eagle gargoyles jutting out of the building on the corners of the sixty-first floor.

If you had *very* powerful binoculars—plus fairy sight— you might notice the unusual nests nestled on top of the steel beaks of the gargoyles. These nests belong to the Avian fairies, a breed that is half bird and half winged fairy; they hatch from eggs, and downy feathers cover their wings. Accustomed to staggering heights, Avian fairies rarely descend to the ground, spending their days instead amidst the clouds, coasting from skyscraper to skyscraper.

The Liberty Bell

This two-thousand-pound symbol of American freedom hangs in Philadelphia, the country's first capital. Made mostly from copper and tin, the bell was originally cast in 1752 in London and shipped to Pennsylvania.

You've likely heard about the famous crack up the side of the bell; no one can decide exactly how many times it has cracked and been repaired or why it kept cracking in the first place. I suspect that the family of fairies who've lived inside that crack for centuries *might* have something to do with it. After all, if someone kept trying to seal up your house, wouldn't you get mad and do something about it too?

On the Question of
Photographing Fairies

Every once in a while, someone claims to have taken the world's first photograph of a fairy. These photographers and their pictures are *always* proven to be fakes. Likewise, as you saw in the encyclopedia entry in Tale No. 7, ball lightning has *never* been photographed, causing many people to call the phenomenon a myth.

Consider the following famous story as well, about the so-called Cottingley fairy photographs, taken by two young cousins in England in the early 1900s. Elsie Wright, sixteen, and Frances Griffiths, ten, presented their families with five photos of themselves with tiny winged creatures taken in the forested Cottingley Glen, near Wright's home.

Many experts—including Sir Arthur Conan Doyle, the author of the Sherlock Holmes detective mysteries—examined the Cottingley photographs and proclaimed that they were indeed pictures of fairies. After sixty long years of ill-earned fame, Elsie and Frances admitted that the photos had been a hoax; the Cottingley "fairies" in the photos had been simple paper cutouts.

If you have plans to take your camera out into your own backyard to document fairy activity, prepare to be disappointed. I'm sorry to be the bearer of bad news, but no fairy has ever been successfully photographed and no fairy ever will—and this includes the Pyrofairies behind ball lightning.

You've probably been taught in school that there are only three forms of matter: gas, liquid, and solid. Fairies are made from a fourth form of matter, the composition of which cannot be understood by humans or photographed. It has something to do with the particular way fairy matter reflects light, and this applies to all breeds—from goblins to mermaids to the winged species.

Now that we've settled that, let's move on.

Fairies and Animals

All fairy breeds have long and storied histories with animals.

As you will see in the next story, stables are one of the most likely places to encounter fairy activity today: winged fairies often live with birds who build nests in barn eaves, and help themselves to eggs from under the warm feathered rumps of hens. One tiny type of fairy—the Equine fairy—makes its own barn nests out of horsehair and hay.

If you own a horse or pony, look closely at its mane or tail on May Day; you may notice tiny white flowers hidden in the coarse hair. Fairies love to decorate horses with flowers. They also leave hollyhocks in the southwest corner of horse stalls on Christmas Eve; this supposedly protects the horses from cold winter winds and illness.

Fairies also love most dogs, whether wild or domesticated. If your dog naps a great deal, it may be because a fairy has "adopted" it and sings lullabies to it throughout the day. Dogs with large upright ears—like German shepherds or French bulldogs—are great favorites, because they can hear a fairy calling from outside.

Long life in a dog is another sign that it has been adopted by a fairy, who probably cast a long-life enchantment over the

animal when it was a puppy. When dogs do eventually die, their bones and graves are very holy to winged fairies and are protected with spells against roaming trolls.

On the other hand, cats are far too independent and shrewd for fairies' liking. If your cat tends to sneeze a great deal, a pesty fairy may be blowing dust and pollen into the cat's nose to annoy it. If you want to protect your cat from fairies, simply roll up a sock and put it under the cat's bed, and the problems will disappear in no time.

Not many people know this, but all inchworms and ladybugs are fairy pets—every single one of them. If you see either of these creatures in your house, it's best to shuttle it outside on a sheet of paper as quickly as possible, lest a fairy come looking for it and think that you have stolen it.

On that note, never put a found inchworm or ladybug into a cage; it will die very quickly, and you will certainly make an enemy of the fairy who owns it.

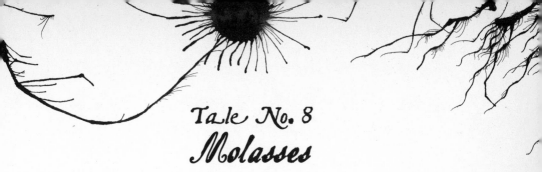

Tale No. 8
Molasses

The bedroom door swung open.

"What is that smell?" demanded Edie's mother, her nostrils quivering as she sniffed about.

"What smell?" said Edie innocently as she lay in bed, her sheet and blanket pulled up to her chin.

"You know what smell," said her mother, narrowing her eyes, and then she whipped the blanket off the bed.

"Aha!" she cried. "I knew I smelled those filthy riding boots. Take them off this instant. Just wait until your father hears about this."

Edie sat up, pulled off the black leather boots, and dropped them on the floor. Some brown clumps fell off onto the rug. Edie's mother looked horrified.

"Horse manure!" she cried, burrowing her hands into her pillowy hips. "Strip that bed down right away, and when you're done, take those boots into the basement and run them under the faucet."

Edie, who was ten, did as she was told. When she came back upstairs, her mother was rocking away rather aggressively in Edie's rocking chair. She tapped her fingers on the wood armrests as Edie made up the bed with fresh sheets.

"Now you listen to me," her mother said. "You're spending far too much time at the stable. First it was twice a week after school. Then every day after school, and then on weekends too. And now, going in the morning before school and wearing your boots to bed? It's too much. The last straw, in fact. Your father will be aghast."

"So don't tell him," Edie advised. "And anyway, you said that I could go as much as I wanted as long as I got good marks." This was guaranteed to stump her mother, for Edie was excelling in her classes.

Her mother stopped rocking. "It's not good for a child to have so little sleep," she countered. "Especially a young lady."

Edie climbed back into bed.

"Not everyone needs ten hours of sleep each night, plus an afternoon nap, you know," she said slyly, for that was exactly the sort of schedule her mother kept.

"What a mouth!" said her mother, standing up. "I'll rinse it out with soap; oh, yes I will. Just wait until your father hears about this." She marched to the door. "Don't let me catch you putting your boots on those clean bedclothes. Go straight to sleep."

And she shut the door behind her.

When Edie could no longer hear her mother's footsteps in the hallway, she got up and placed her riding boots next to her bed. That way she could literally just step right into them on her way to the stable in the morning. She was already secretly wearing her riding clothes under her pajamas. Edie was the sort of girl who hated wasting even one extra second on anything.

The clock on her bedside table said 10 p.m. Only another seven hours and fifteen minutes until Edie would be in the stable, a block from her house.

It took a while to get comfortable, wearing all of those clothes, but eventually she closed her eyes and went to sleep.

⚘ ⚘ ⚘

It was dark when she got there, as usual; during winter in New York City, the sun doesn't rise until later, when half the city's inhabitants are already rushing to work or to school. Edie could barely make out the familiar sign swinging above the entrance:

The Claremont Riding Academy consisted of a small, sawdust-strewn indoor ring and a vast, rickety stable on many levels; the horses walked from floor to floor on spiraled ramps. You could have a lesson in the ring, or, if the weather cooperated, you could take one of the horses for a trail ride in Central Park, which was just blocks away.

A soothing calm filled the stable early in the morning. Usually there was the sound of sleepy school horses chewing hay in their stalls, their buckets tapping gently against the wooden walls; occasionally one of them would stamp or neigh, but these were nice noises and Edie liked being in a pocket of the country hidden away in a big city. The horses had reassuring fairy-tale names like Winifred and Gandalf and Bruno.

Edie rode an old swaybacked gelding called Molasses. Actually, Molasses wasn't officially Edie's horse; he belonged to the school. But no one else was allowed to ride or groom Molasses. He and Edie belonged to each other, that was a fact. If you tried to put a saddle on Molasses and you weren't Edie, you would get a nip. Molasses might be eighteen and mostly used up, but he still had quite a set of chompers.

On this morning, however, there was not a lovely calm in the stable when Edie arrived. Instead, there was something anxious and odd and chaotic happening. The grooms ran from stall to stall, carrying blankets and buckets; a few of them stood in the middle of the stable and argued.

Edie tugged on the sleeve of her favorite groom, a tiny, tough former jockey named Pinkney.

"What's going on?" she asked.

"It's bedlam," Pinkney told her. "When we got here half an hour ago, we found all of the horses exhausted and sweating, like someone had been riding them all night."

"All of them?" asked Edie incredulously. There were nearly fifty horses in the stable.

"Every single one," said Pinkney, rubbing his temples with his thumbs.

"Even Molasses?" cried Edie, but she didn't wait for Pinkney's answer. She ran to Molasses's stall and rolled the door aside. The horse's wet body steamed in the cold winter-morning air and his head dropped with tiredness.

"We can't figure it out," said Pinkney as he followed Edie into the stall and helped her throw a blanket over Molasses's back. "All of the doors were locked. Nothing was out of place. But just look at this horse. He's practically a pile of soap."

He stopped talking for a minute, and then he said, "That's strange."

"What's strange?" said Edie, wishing Pinkney would leave. She wanted to soothe the horse in private.

"Look at that," Pinkney said, pointing at Molasses's legs. Mud spatters covered them, all the way up to the horse's chest and belly. Edie wiped one leg down and the towel turned desert-colored, a deep maroon. It could have been from the surface of Mars, it was that color. Then she gently picked up one of the gelding's hooves; sandy dirt caked the bottom.

"There isn't any sandy red dirt in Central Park," Pinkney said, rubbing his temples again. "Last time I checked, anyway. I bet we'll never get to the bottom of it, not ever," he added unhelpfully, and shambled out of the stall on his bandy little legs.

Edie tenderly chiseled the mud from the horse's hooves. And while she did this, she imagined someone else riding her beloved Molasses and felt a green flash of betrayal.

"I can't believe that you went riding with someone else," she scolded, standing up. "How could you?"

Molasses just blinked at her and then slowly swung his head in the other direction.

Edie felt ashamed then.

"I take it back," she said quickly. She pressed her nose against the horse's muzzle and breathed in his patient, hay-scented breath.

When she was sure that Molasses was warm and clean and safe again, Edie left for school.

There was no question of riding that afternoon; when Edie walked by the stable after school, a handwritten sign hung on the closed front gates.

Closed for Maintenance

Which really meant that the grooms were letting the horses rest after their mysterious midnight run.

The next morning, just before dawn, the sign was still up. Edie pounded on the big wooden front doors until footsteps approached on the other side.

"Closed for repairs; come back tomorrow," said Pinkney's voice from inside.

"Wait—it's me, Edie," said Edie.

"Oh," said Pinkney, opening the door. He looked like he needed a drink. "Get in here quick and help us out, will you?"

They marched through the ring and up the stable ramps.

"It happened again," Pinkney told her, his brow covered in sweat, even though their breath made white clouds in the cold morning air. "We even left a groom overnight as a lookout—Little Burl. But this morning when we got here, it took five cups of coffee to get him awake and talking again—coffee, and a few smacks. It was like he'd been drugged or something. And all the poor horses have been ridden within an inch of their lives."

Molasses was a wreck. Mud covered his legs and clogged his hooves again, and this time thistles and burs and tiny purple flowers knotted his mane and tail. He bucked up several times when Edie tried to comb them out; there was nothing left to do but pull out the scissors.

"Oh, he looks awful," Edie cried when she and Pinkney finished the emergency haircut. Humiliated, Molasses turned around and faced the wall.

"Pinkney, where are there *thistles* around here?" Edie wondered, holding up the sad tendrils of mane. "I mean, thistles and flowers in New York City, in the middle of winter?"

The jockey examined the matted horsehair.

"These remind me of fine heather," he said, fingering the flowers. "The kind that you only find covering the great moors in Scotland; they turn the whole countryside purple." He left to tend to the other horses.

Edie frowned. Someone was giving Molasses a very hard time, and if she didn't do something, the horse could be ridden to lameness—or worse. Clearly the grooms couldn't be relied upon to catch the culprit.

She buried her schoolbag in the hay in the stall's corner and hid in the girls' bathroom. She stayed there all day and into the evening and then into the night, until the last groom left and closed the front gates with a clatter.

Edie tiptoed out of the bathroom toward Molasses's stall.

A long, low whistle came from one of the stalls and Edie froze. Goose bumps rose on her arms. But then the whistle turned into a tune, sort of an off-key "Yankee Doodle," and Edie relaxed: the grooms had left Little Burl there again to watch over the horses.

She slipped into Molasses's stall and kept watch from the scratchy pile of straw in the corner.

The stable creaked in a midnight sort of way and cold air seeped up through the floorboards. Every few minutes Edie's chin nodded down to her chest. Soon Little Burl stopped whistling "Yankee Doodle," and Edie knew that his chin must be nodding to his chest too. She pinched herself to stay awake.

Nod, pinch, nod.

But as Edie was about to nod off for the hundredth time,

a rustling sound came from the corridor. She jerked her head back, held her breath, and listened.

It was a faint noise at first, but it grew louder; it sounded like little feet scurrying across the floorboards.

Mice, Edie concluded with disgust, drawing her knees to her chest. Molasses shifted uneasily as the mice ran down the hall toward the stalls in the back.

"Hey!" shouted Little Burl. "What the—"

But he didn't finish his sentence; instead came the sound of a body falling onto the floor, followed by deep, rattling snores.

And then the scurrying came back again, toward Edie's stall.

She stood up and grabbed at the first weapon she could reach: a rubber currycomb.

Suddenly a face peeked into the stall, a very ugly little face. It looked like a clenched fist or a newborn baby's face, all wrinkled up, its eyes almost closed. Pointed ears jutted from the sides of its head; its mouth curled into a devilish grin.

The creature stared at Edie and Edie stared back; then suddenly it darted into the stall on long, spider-like legs. Those awful legs and its pencil-line arms made the creature seem sprawling and gangly, even though it stood only about a foot high. Molasses reared up, baring his teeth, his eyes rolling backward.

Edie screamed and threw the currycomb as hard as she could. It hit the spindly creature's head with a rubbery *doink*, knocking it over backward.

She held her breath, terrified of what would happen next.

Edie was right to worry; after all, pixies have unpredictable tempers under the best of circumstances.

⚜ ⚜ ⚜

Everyone knows about pixies; even Shakespeare made one into a character. Surely you've heard of Puck from A Midsummer Night's Dream, a prankster who turns people's heads into donkey heads and other generally naughty but amusing things.

Like many fairy breeds, pixies originally came from England, but when they migrated, they mostly tended to move to France, since they are very fond of cheese and you can't find better cheese than French cheese. Not many pixies have made America their home, so I was quite surprised when I first heard about this New York City–based population. Pixies usually hate overcrowding, and the few American ones usually live on the great western plains and mountains.

All pixies live near stables. They love horses, and for centuries pixies have famously "borrowed" steeds

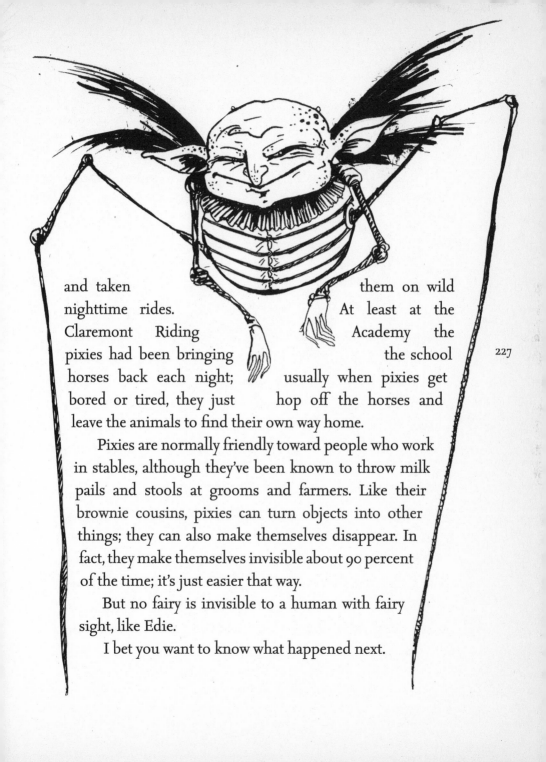

and taken nighttime rides. Claremont Riding Academy the pixies had been bringing horses back each night; bored or tired, they just them on wild At least at the the school usually when pixies get hop off the horses and leave the animals to find their own way home.

Pixies are normally friendly toward people who work in stables, although they've been known to throw milk pails and stools at grooms and farmers. Like their brownie cousins, pixies can turn objects into other things; they can also make themselves disappear. In fact, they make themselves invisible about 90 percent of the time; it's just easier that way.

But no fairy is invisible to a human with fairy sight, like Edie.

I bet you want to know what happened next.

Both Edie and the pixie leaped for Molasses at the same time.

The pixie landed first, and Edie threw herself on top of the creature and tried to throw it to the ground. But the pixie grabbed Molasses's shorn mane and dug its feet into the horse's sides and Molasses shot out of the stall like a racehorse at the starting gate.

Down the ramp, around three times, through the ring, and out the front door: Edie gripped the horse's mane and found herself hugging the fairy as they both held on for dear life. And then Edie realized that they weren't alone: all fifty school horses—each carrying a screeching pixie—pounded out of the Claremont Riding Academy onto West 89th Street and headed toward Central Park.

Molasses crashed through a thorny hedge and galloped across a field; he headed for a huge tree. Edie screamed and ducked, her eyes squeezed shut. But they didn't hit the tree, and Molasses ran even harder and the pixie squealed with glee. Suddenly they were going so fast that the trees and skyscrapers and other buildings surrounding the park became a black smear and the city seemed to flatten itself out.

Then Edie realized that they weren't even in the city anymore: the whole herd of school horses was galloping across *water*, a lot of water—maybe even an ocean.

The pixie whooped and shrieked and a terrified Edie dug her legs even harder into Molasses's side, which only made the horse go faster yet. The tears streaming out of Edie's eyes cut salty paths straight back across the sides of her face, over the tops of her ears, and into her hair. After a while the horizon glowed blue in front of them and the herd tore into the daylight, the sea shining silver below their hooves.

And suddenly they were on land again.

Edie had seen pictures of deserts before, but this desert didn't look anything like those pictures. Instead of gentle curves and hills of silky sand, this desert was made from vast, packed-sand steppes that cut into the horizon on all sides. The horses fanned out, gasping for breath, white foam hanging like string from their mouths.

One of the pixies threw something onto the ground, a leather ball: it was odd, hard, misshapen, as though it had been left to wither in the sun for years.

All fifty pixies screamed in delight and suddenly they held big wooden mallets, grasped from the thin, dusty air; they kicked the horses, and like vultures swarming to a carcass, they all attacked the ball at once.

A savage game of desert polo had begun.

Mallets cut through the air like swinging swords, sometimes hitting the ball, sometimes knocking a pixie down under the hooves of the stampede, sometimes *thwacking* a horse on the back of the head or even in the face. There were no goals, no rules, no teams; there was only an endless, anarchic chase. Molasses bucked and reared, but the pixie kept him in the game. A mallet smacked Edie on the knee and another hit her side and black bruises swelled up immediately.

Then the ball rolled near Molasses, and suddenly they were surrounded by raised mallets and grinning little fist-tight faces.

Edie screamed, certain that she was about to be pummeled to death. Her pixie clubbed the ball away just in time and the bloodied mob galloped after it.

That's when Edie saw that the ball wasn't a ball at all.

It was a *goat's head*.

Edie fainted and fell off Molasses, and then there was only the sound of the herd galloping away.

A low-hanging gray haze hid the sun, but it was still hot—
very hot, in fact—and sweat drenched Edie's hair by the time
she opened her eyes again. The horses were far away by then;
Molasses was gone too, mixed in with the herd, which kicked
up a tornado of dusty sand wherever it went.

Edie watched the polo storm move farther and farther
away until it was a wisp on the horizon—and then it was
gone.

She was all alone in that strange desert.

Edie tried to cry, but she was too dried up inside and the
tears wouldn't come.

Then she tried to walk, but she kept ending up back at the same spot, and so she gave that up too.

There was nothing left to do but sit on that hard ground and wait for more nothing to do.

For some reason, the words to Little Burl's stable tune kept running through Edie's mind. She swallowed a few times and began to sing to herself:

> Yankee Doodle went to town
> Riding on a pony
> Stuck a feather in his cap
> And called it macaroni.

Edie laughed, and it was sort of a crazy laugh, and then she sang the song again. What else could she do?

Nothing, nothing at all.

So she sang it again and again and then she stood up and shouted it at the top of her lungs.

Suddenly her words came back to her in an eerie echo, growing louder and louder like an approaching freight train until the ground trembled with the sound.

Edie threw herself down on the ground and curled up on her side. She lay that way for a long time, wondering what it would be like to be lost forever. How did people who were "lost forever" spend their time? Were there still hours and days and

minutes? Would she be lonely, or would she get used to it here?

Soon it grew dark again, and it got cold too, as it always does in the desert at night; Edie shivered and curled up tighter, and then she fell asleep.

Someone was washing her face with a rough, wet cloth.

"That hurts," she protested, pushing it away. She opened her eyes and blinked. The room came into focus.

Her room.

Edie was back in her bed at home.

"Your face is *filthy*," said Edie's mother, standing over her. "Where on earth have you *been*? I can't believe that it's possible for a young lady to get so dirty. Just *wait* until your father hears about this." She dipped the cloth into a bowl of water and scrubbed Edie's forehead.

"Stop it!" Edie cried. "You're scrubbing too hard."

"Dirt, dirt, everywhere," said her mother, washing even harder. "Dirt and mud and manure. We must get you clean. We *must*."

Edie covered up her face with her hands, but the cloth kept on rubbing and dabbing, and when Edie opened her eyes again, her mother was gone and so was her bedroom. She wasn't home after all.

She was still in the desert.

Molasses stood over her, licking her face with his rough, warm tongue.

Edie squinted up at him. The horse had come back for her. The pixie was gone; maybe abandoned in another part of the desert, like Edie had been, or maybe smashed in the polo stampede.

Molasses nudged her with his muzzle and Edie stood up on wobbly legs. It took her a while to get up on his back, but he was patient and eventually she managed.

They trotted off across the dry desert steppes, and then

Molasses went faster and faster and finally broke into a gallop, and soon water splashed up on their legs.

They were running back across the sea.

Edie wrapped her arms around the horse's neck and buried her face in his shorn mane, feeling his powerful muscles moving beneath his hide. Then the ground was hard under his hooves again and Molasses slowed down and clip-clopped up West 89th Street to the Claremont Riding Academy: through the sawdust-strewn ring, up the ramp, down the corridor, and back into his stall.

When Pinkney and the other grooms arrived at the stable just after dawn, they were astonished to find the girl still fast asleep on her horse's back.

You may have noticed that the name "Edie" sounds remarkably like the name "Edythe."

I would have given you a gold star for being so observant.

This is indeed my own story.

"Edie" used to be my nickname. This experience happened to me when I was ten years old.

Molasses was the only horse that returned to the stable

that night. All of the other horses vanished. I guess that the pixies decided to keep them for good. For all I know, the horses are still with those pixies, playing ferocious games of desert polo—or someplace else entirely. Antarctica, or maybe the North Pole. Perhaps leaping over waterfalls in the Amazon jungle.

Reporters wrote articles for years about the disappearance of the forty-nine Claremont Academy horses, and they wrote articles about me too. Scholars said that my description of the pixie desert sounded very much like the steppes in Afghanistan, and they wondered how I knew so much about the geography there.

At first they said that I had quite an imagination.

But then, as I got older and refused to take back my story, they said that I was crazy—or worse, a liar.

So I started to gather information about the fairy world and report on its many inhabitants. I traveled across the globe many times and talked to hundreds of people who had encounters like mine. People like Daisy and Olive; like George, Felix, and Imogene; like Annabelle, Mirabelle, and Lucius.

I wanted to prove to the world that I had been right.

Yet to this day, despite countless testimonies and overwhelming evidence, most people still do not believe in fairies.

But I know that you know better.

Molasses lived for another seven years after our adventure.

The Claremont Riding Academy was over a hundred years old when it closed in 2007.

And the pixies never returned.

The Future of Fairies

The world is changing in many ways. Pollution is getting worse, and the atmosphere is getting warmer. Cities are getting more and more crowded, and spilling farther into the countryside. All of these changes affect how fairies live and whether they will be able to survive in the long run.

When more forests get chopped down, that means fewer homes for brownies and other tree-dwelling fairies.

When chemicals and trash contaminate oceans, rivers, and streams, there are fewer livable habitats for the Lorelei and other mermaids.

When big companies drill for oil and minerals, they often destroy underground dwarf mines and villages, forcing dwarves to search in vain for new homes.

As you have seen in this book, most fairy breeds are adaptable and have carved out places for themselves in the modern world. But as you also know, fairies are very closely tied to nature—much more than humans seem to be—and the continued destruction of the environment may put fairies in the same category as dinosaurs:

Extinct.

Many of the more rare and more fragile species are already dying out.

The loss of fairies would be tragic for humans. While fairies clearly have their darker side, they also make us appreciate the beauty of trees and flowers and look for what is special about our everyday surroundings.

They remind us to *always* look twice, that first impressions and appearances can be deceptive.

They teach us that surprises may lie behind closed doors and set an example when it comes to treasuring animals.

Each of us can do our part to make sure that fairies always have a place in our world.

Start in your own home. To help the environment, make sure that your family recycles things like newspapers, cans, and plastic bottles. Don't waste food, and don't let faucets drip. Never litter, and if you see trash on the ground, throw it away, even if it didn't belong to you. Plant a tree with your parents or your class at school.

Doing little things like this every day will help

keep the earth clean and preserve the fairy realm—and ensure that future generations will share the world with these magical creatures.

Just make sure that you teach your own children and grandchildren and great-grandchildren the penny trick about telling a good fairy from a bad one.

After all, you are now officially an expert in the ways of modern fairies, dwarves, goblins, and other nasties.

The End

Acknowledgments

The author and illustrator wish to extend special thanks to Elissa Lumley, without whom this happy collaboration would not exist.

The author would like to thank the following people, whose help with this project was invaluable and highly appreciated: Erin Clarke, Nancy Hinkel, Kate Lee, Christine Bauch, Gregory Macek, Caitlin Crounse, Jessica Sailer, Sara Just, and the staffs of Norwood and Sant Ambroeus for tolerating hours of research and writing on their distinguished premises.

Lesley M. M. Blume spent much of her childhood sitting in her backyard, willing fairies to appear. These days, she is an author and journalist based in New York City. Her critically acclaimed books for children include *Cornelia and the Audacious Escapades of the Somerset Sisters*, *The Rising Star of Rusty Nail*, and *Tennyson*, which the *Chicago Tribune* praised for its "brilliant, unusual writing."

You can learn more about her at www.lesleymmblume.com.

David Foote envisions the world through a fantastical black-and-white looking glass.

He is a fine artist, filmmaker, and animator who left his hometown of Caracas, Venezuela, at eighteen to study at the Parsons School of Design in New York City, where he currently lives. *Modern Fairies, Dwarves, Goblins & Other Nasties* is his first children's book.

Visit him on the Web at www.davidfootestudio.com.